W9-BZB-450

The Adventures of

Erasmus Twiddle

Grmkville's famous & talented Not-Detective

By Eric Laster

Illustrated by Amy Abshier

Simon & Schuster Books for Young Readers

New York London Toronto Sydney Singapore

SIMON & SCHUSTER BOOKS FOR YOUNG READERS
An imprint of Simon & Schuster Children's Publishing Division
1230 Avenue of the Americas, New York, New York 10020
Text copyright © 2001 by Eric Laster
Illustrations copyright © 2001 by Amy Abshier

All rights reserved, including the right of reproduction in whole or in part in any form.
SIMON & SCHUSTER BOOKS FOR YOUNG READERS is a trademark of Simon & Schuster.

Book design by Jennifer Reyes and Anahid Hamparian
The text of this book is set in 12-point Goudy Old Style.
The illustrations are rendered in pen and ink.
Printed in the United States of America
2 4 6 8 10 9 7 5 3 1
Library of Congress Cataloging-in-Publication Data
Laster, Eric.
The adventures of Erasmus Twiddle : Grmkville's famous & talented not-detective / by
Eric Laster ; illustrated by Amy Abshier.—1st ed.
p. cm.
Summary: In the small town of Grmkville, young "not-detective" Erasmus Twiddle solves
the Case of the Missing Rubber Chicken, the Case of the Soggy Dumpling, and other mysteries.
ISBN 0-689-84245-7
[1. Humorous stories. 2. Mystery and detective stories.] I. Abshier, Amy, ill. II. Title.
PZ7.L32955 Ad 2001
[Fic]—dc21   00-046322

FIRST
EDITION

For Kate
E. L.

To Ricky, just because
A. A.

Acknowledgments

Thanks to Tracey Adams, Sam Pinkus and Evva Pryor at McIntosh & Otis, Inc., Stephanie Owens Lurie at Dutton, and everybody at Simon & Schuster, especially Amy-Hampton Knight, editor extraordinaire, for all your insight, guidance, and support in the birthing of this book.

A big thank you to Anne Winter and the Reading Reptile in Kansas City, without whom this never would have happened. To my mom and dad, my amazing family, and all my dear friends—thank you for all the love and support you've given me over the years.

Contents

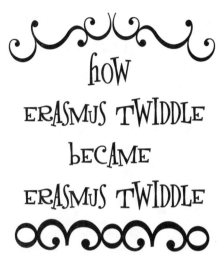

hOW ERASMUS TWIDDLE bECAME ERASMUS TWIDDLE

Everybody knows that babies are special. You never hear a mother say, "Would you look at my baby? Ugh. This is not a very special baby. No, sir. This is the most un-special baby I've ever seen." You never hear a mother say this because mothers—along with everybody else—know that babies are special.

So it should come as no surprise that not all that long ago, in the not-very-large town of Grmkville, a baby boy was born who was special in all the ways that babies are special. Except that this baby proved special in a special way. One day his mother, Mrs. Twiddle, misplaced a finger puppet. She was searching for this finger puppet when the baby pointed at a moose. It was not really a moose, just a bunch of wire and canvas that had been painted to look like a moose. It was really a moose magazine rack.

"Goo!" said baby Erasmus.

1

"Not goo," said Mrs. Twiddle. "A moose magazine rack."

But baby Erasmus did not listen. He kept pointing at the moose magazine rack and saying "Goo!" And Mrs. Twiddle did not listen. She searched everywhere for her finger puppet—everywhere except the moose magazine rack.

"Goo!" insisted baby Erasmus, wiggling a foot at the moose magazine rack.

"All right, all right," said Mrs. Twiddle.

And guess what Mrs. Twiddle found when she searched the moose magazine rack? No, not that. No, not that either. Fine, I'll tell you. She found her finger puppet (and a bit of sticky substance, or "goo"). Mrs. Twiddle thought this was just one of life's funny little coincidences—Erasmus finding her finger puppet. But a week later she misplaced her banana bandana, a nifty piece of yellow clothing she liked very much. She searched everywhere for her banana bandana but could not find it. Erasmus waved his arms at a bowl of fruit that was not a bowl of fruit at all. It was just a bowl of plastic that looked like fruit and was supposed to be pretty.

"Gah!" said baby Erasmus.

"Not gah," said Mrs. Twiddle. "Plastic fruit. It's not really fruit at all but it's very pretty."

Then Mrs. Twiddle remembered the goo-finger puppet episode. She lifted up the bowl of fruit that was not fruit at all and—lo and behold—there was her banana bandana (but no "gah"). It became clear to Mrs. Twiddle that Erasmus had a knack for solving little mysteries. Actually, he had a knack for solving big and medium-sized mysteries, too. It did not matter if an item were lost or stolen; if it had mysteriously disappeared, Erasmus Twiddle would find it.

Well, Erasmus is no longer a baby. Over the years he has found many things for many people, and he has solved mysteries of every size and shape. I suppose I could tell you a great deal about our hero. For instance, I could tell you that he is not a detective, he is just curious and likes to solve mysteries. I could also tell you that he is famous in the town of Grmkville for solving mysteries.

"I do not like it when people ask me if I'm a detective," says Erasmus Twiddle. "Anyone can be a detective. All they have to do is send four bottle caps, three proof-of-purchase seals from their favorite cereal, two AA batteries, and one rattlesnake skin to P.O. Box 12345, and soon they will receive their detective license in the mail."

Erasmus is a nice boy who gets a bit grinchy sometimes. This is not unusual. Everybody gets grinchy sometimes. How old is Erasmus Twiddle? Perhaps he is not much older than you. Perhaps he is not older than you at all.

"I have read about the famous detective, Sherlock Holmes," says Erasmus Twiddle, "and I once considered calling myself Erasmus Holmes or Sherlock Twiddle. I thought I could borrow parts of his name so that people would know

3

I'm not a detective but could still help them if they had . . . well, if they had an exploding donkey or something. In the end, though, I stuck with Erasmus Twiddle. I don't think my mother would have liked me to change my name."

You see how much there is to know about our hero. By the way, Erasmus is not a three-legged goat who can recite the Japanese alphabet backwards while balancing a cane on the tip of his nose and dancing the Charleston. You probably knew this already, but I thought I should tell it to you all the same. You should be thankful that Erasmus is not a goat with so many talents. I do not speak Japanese. If our hero were a goat and he started reciting the Japanese alphabet backwards, I would not understand a word he was saying. I am trying to tell you that I cannot possibly tell you everything there is to know about our hero. The best way to get to know Erasmus is to read this book. It is very entertaining, believe me. It is perhaps the best book ever written on a Monday. And when you have finished reading it, not only will you feel very smart, but you will be able to amaze your friends and their pets by telling them much more than just how Erasmus Twiddle became Erasmus Twiddle, Grmkville's famous and talented not-detective.

the case of the RUBBER CHICKEN

1

A rubber chicken is a curious thing. You cannot bounce a rubber chicken the way you can bounce a rubber ball. You cannot stretch a rubber chicken the way you can stretch a rubber band. You cannot eat a rubber chicken the way you can eat a regular chicken. A rubber chicken cannot lay eggs or cluck or scratch the dirt the way regular chickens lay eggs and cluck and scratch the dirt. In fact, a rubber chicken cannot do anything but flop around. And even this it cannot do on its own. You have to make it flop. You shake the rubber chicken and it flops. It looks funny when it flops and it might make you laugh, but remember, you are making yourself laugh. You are the one flopping the rubber chicken.

So it is strange that Erasmus Twiddle, our famous and talented not-detective from the not-very-large town of

Grmkville, should be asked by Mr. Jax to recover his stolen rubber chicken. It is even stranger that someone has stolen Mr. Jax's rubber chicken because a rubber chicken cannot do anything and is not worth very much money.

"Someone has stolen my rubber chicken!" exclaims Mr. Jax, who stands at the tippy top of a ladder, polishing a bronze thingamabob that sits on a tippy-top shelf in his room of doodads.

"That is very curious," replies Erasmus Twiddle.

"Very curious, indeed," says Mr. Jax. "My rubber chicken means a great deal to me."

"Yes, of course," says Erasmus Twiddle.

Everyone in Grmkville knows how much the rubber chicken means to Mr. Jax. This is because he is always telling people. He paints large signs for all of Grmkville to see: **MR. JAX LOVES HIS RUBBER CHICKEN.** And when he is out and about, grocery shopping and such, he says things like, "Hello, Snoots Waterford. How's the pork chop today? Boy, do I love my rubber chicken." Or he says, "Hello, Dotty Polka. Lovely weather we're having. Gee, I love my rubber chicken." Erasmus Twiddle has often wondered how a rubber chicken could mean so much to a person.

"I don't think I could ever care so much for a rubber chicken," whispers Erasmus Twiddle, "but that is neither here nor there. It is not right to steal anything from anybody."

This is very true. A famous and talented not-detective must try just as hard to recover a stolen rubber chicken as he would to recover a case of stolen jewels.

"Did you say something?" asks Mr. Jax.

"Um, yes," says Erasmus Twiddle. "It might help my investigation if you could tell me . . . well, what is the purpose of a rubber chicken?"

"Ah," says Mr. Jax, "a rubber chicken is special precisely because it has no purpose. It is utterly useless!"

"I see," says Erasmus Twiddle, even though he doesn't see at all.

"Take this thingamabob, for instance," says Mr. Jax. "It is my precious thingamabob and it does nothing whatsoever. Have you ever heard of a thingamabob that did anything? Who has heard of such a thing? Preposterous!"

If you look closely at Mr. Jax's house you will see that it is filled with useless objects: a plastic whatsis, a metal whodoyoucallit, a wooden hootenanny.

"I am a collector," says Mr. Jax. "I collect collectibles." And with that, he hops off his ladder and points to a broken window. "There, that is where the thief entered my house to steal my rubber chicken!"

"Yes," says Erasmus Twiddle. "I noticed the broken window some time ago, as would any not-detective worthy of being a not-detective."

"Right," says Mr. Jax. "How silly of me."

"I would like to take a closer look at that window, if I may," says Erasmus.

And take a closer look at the window he does. There is a large hole in the center of it and little bits of glass on the carpet and many more bits on the ground outside. There are no bricks, rocks or pebbles anywhere to be seen, so it is impossible to know what was used to break the window.

"Hmm," says a thoughtful Erasmus Twiddle. "That is a broken window, all right."

"I told you," says Mr. Jax. "I came home from collecting collectibles and found the window broken just as you see it now. I didn't know what it could mean. I was sure that if someone had broken the window by accident, there would be a note explaining what had happened. But there was no note. And then I saw that my rubber chicken was missing from its place between the mugamug-whatcha and the hopping huh-huhmajig."

"What time did you leave the house to collect collectibles?" asks Erasmus Twiddle, acting every bit the professional not-detective.

"Three o'clock," answers Mr. Jax. "At least that was the time on my collectible grandfather clock there in the corner."

Mr. Jax points to a large clock standing in the corner of the room. It does not look like an ordinary clock. If you look quickly at it you will think there is an old man with gray hair standing in the corner. But look closer and you will see that instead of eyes, nose, and mouth—instead of a regular grandfather face—the old man has a face of numbers. Why, it is the face of a clock, and his long tie swings back and forth, back and forth, ticking out the seconds!

"That really is my grandfather," says Mr. Jax. "I had him made into a clock."

Perhaps you think it strange that Mr. Jax had his grandfather made into a clock. Perhaps it is strange and perhaps it isn't. Different people do different things and it is possible that Mr. Jax's grandfather wanted to be a clock—that way he could make sure Mr. Jax would not be late for appointments. (Mr. Jax was always late for appointments with his grandfather.)

"You are very thoughtful to have made your grandfather into a clock," says Erasmus Twiddle, even though he does not think it thoughtful at all. "Now what time did you return home from collecting collectibles to find your rubber chicken missing?"

"Well, um . . . three o'clock," answers Mr. Jax. "My grandfather is broken. I have been meaning to have him fixed, but there are not many people qualified to work on such a collectible clock, you know."

Sure enough, if you look at Mr. Jax's grandfather, you will see that he still says the time is three o'clock. This is not helpful, not helpful at all, because it means that Mr. Jax has no idea what time his rubber chicken was stolen. It would be helpful to know such a thing.

"Yes, it would," whispers Erasmus Twiddle. "But I must do my best. It isn't the business of famous and talented not-detectives to complain. It is the business of famous and talented not-detectives to recover stolen rubber chickens."

"Did you say something?" asks Mr. Jax.

"Yes," says Erasmus. "I would like to know where and when you last saw your rubber chicken."

"Yesterday morning in this very room," replies Mr. Jax. "I took it from the shelf and flopped it around. It was very funny."

But Mr. Jax does not look as if he thinks it was very funny.

10

He does not look as if he thinks anything in the world was ever funny. "Please," says Mr. Jax, "I do not care who stole my rubber chicken or why they stole it. I only want it back. I would give this roomful of doodads to have my rubber chicken returned to me."

"You will not have to give away your roomful of doodads," says Erasmus Twiddle, who is thinking that he would not know what to do with a roomful of doodads. "And don't worry, Mr. Jax. I'm not a famous and talented not-detective for nothing. I always get my rubber chicken."

2

On weekends when the weather was fine, Mr. Jax often took his rubber chicken out for a walk. I do not mean that the rubber chicken itself did any walking because of course it could not do any walking. One time, though, Mr. Jax put a collar on his beloved rubber bird and attached a leash to the collar. He tried to walk his rubber chicken as a person walks a dog. There he was, strolling along—except that his rubber chicken was dragging on the ground behind him! It got all dirty and scratched and he thought it might be better to carry it instead. So that's what he did. He carried it and, being a very friendly person, flopped it at anybody and everybody he saw. Anybody and everybody he saw was always very polite and acted as if he were not flopping a rubber chicken at all.

The first time anyone in Grmkville saw Mr. Jax flop his

rubber chicken, well, they thought it was funny. But after a while it was not so funny. There are only so many times a man can flop a rubber chicken before he becomes just a man flopping a useless rubber chicken.

"I never thought it was funny," sniffs Henrietta Humphreys, the richest and plumpest lady in Grmkville. "Why, I never thought of rubber chickens at all! I'm far too important to think of such useless things! I must count my money and tell my servants what to do! I have just this minute been telling a servant of mine that he is to think of rubber chickens for me! I pay him to do it, so he does it! This servant informs me that I think it's a shame a grown man like Mr. Jax should be seen flopping a rubber chicken in public! Now away with you!"

"To tell you the truth, which is the only thing worth telling," says Sam the Sidewalk Sweeper, "I never really thought about Mr. Jax's rubber chicken. I do like Mr. Jax, though. He never drops napkins or bottlecaps on the sidewalk and forgets to pick them up. So if he likes his rubber chicken, it's okay by me. Rubber chickens don't hurt anyone. But they don't help anyone either. Like a seeing-eye dog. Now there's an animal that helps people. There's no such thing as a seeing-eye rubber chicken."

"A rubber chicken! Why would anyone want to own a rubber chicken?" ask Abel and Barry and Cindy and Darryl and Evelyn and Farrell and George and Harold and Izzy and Jared and Kevin and Larry and Mo and Nancy and Ollie and Perry and Quinn and Randy and Susan and Terry and Ursula and Valerie and William and Xavier and Yolanda and Zachary.

So you see, no one in Grmkville has ever cared enough about Mr. Jax's rubber chicken to even think about it. This makes it an especially hard case for our famous and talented not-detective because it means that not a single person in all of Grmkville would want to steal Mr. Jax's rubber chicken.

"I am thinking of rubber and of chickens," says Erasmus, who is on his way to school, "and I am wondering who first put the two together. I am also thinking about peanuts and pelicans, which have nothing to do with the mystery of the rubber chicken, but I am thinking of them just the same, so I thought I should mention it."

A famous and talented not-detective must put all the facts of a case in order. He must examine all the clues and think very hard about them.

"Yes," says Erasmus, "and it is strange that the burglar only stole Mr. Jax's rubber chicken when his house is filled with useless objects. Whoever took the rubber chicken must have a specific need for a rubber chicken. But what could that be? A rubber chicken cannot do anything that I know of, except be useless. This is a most puzzling case."

"Hark ye and alas! Where goes thyself?" booms a booming loud voice.

A round little boy wearing suspenders and a bow tie hops out from behind a nearby shrub. Why, it is Andrew Michaels, Erasmus Twiddle's good friend.

"I say, hark! Where doth thee go and wherefore! Peradventure! Alas! Rapscallion!" Andrew is an actor and often talks in this strange way.

"If you mean, where am I going," says Erasmus Twiddle, "I am going to Mrs. Mumuschnitzel's class, the same as you are, Andrew Michaels."

"I'm sorry—who? Andrew who? No, good sir, there be no Andrew here. I am called, by those who calleth me, Lorimar Glutchenpuss." Then, in a normal voice, he explains to his friend: "I thought I should change my name for my acting career. All the best actors have stage names, you see."

"Ah," says Erasmus Twiddle.

"Maybe a not-detective should have a stage name too? It might help you to get cases," suggests Andrew Mich— . . . I mean, Lorimar Glutchenpuss.

"I am already famous as Erasmus Twiddle," says Erasmus Twiddle. "Besides, I don't think my mother would like me to change my name. Did you hear that Mr. Jax's rubber chicken has been stolen?"

"Why, begads!" cries Lorimar Glutchenpuss, and clutches his heart for no apparent reason. "I did not! I forswear I have heard of no such dastardly doings! Alas! Woe is me and I be woe!"

"I don't see why *you* should be woe," says our famous and talented not-detective. "It isn't *your* rubber chicken."

This is very true. But Lorimar Glutchenpuss is an actor and likes to pretend that the misfortunes of others are his own.

"Speaketh to me, fair friend, of this foul tragedy!" booms Lorimar Glutchenpuss. "Oh speaketh of the tragedy of the missing rubber fowl! I am not sure yet what to calleth it."

"Well," says Erasmus, "Mr. Jax's rubber chicken has been stolen and I have no idea who stole it."

"Surely, brave and gallant Twiddle, that is only the short version of the story," declares Lorimar. "For every dastardly doing is a long tale of woe. Pray, telleth me this long tale of woe, you woe-teller, you."

"Well," says a very thoughtful Erasmus Twiddle, who does not know of any long version, "Mr. Jax's rubber chicken has been stolen and I have no idea who stole it."

"Awful, awful," says Lorimar. "Upon this sad day, I have written a soliloquy—which, as you know, fair Twiddle, is just a fancy word for a bunch of stuff said by an actor." And with that, Lorimar Glutchenpuss launches into his soliloquy. Which goes like this:

> *"How sad when chickens go,*
> *Be they of rubber or some other*
> *Stuff. Oh, sad sad chicken, where have you gone?*
> *To hear you cluck no more . . . even though,*
> *Well, you never really clucked anyway, being bird unreal—"*

"Andrew?" interrupts Erasmus. But his good friend does not seem to hear.

"—flopping here and flopping there—" continues Lorimar.

"Lorimar?" says Erasmus, who has just remembered his friend's new name.

"—flopping everywhere without a care, flopped by hand unseen—"

"LORIMAR!"

Lorimar stops and looks around. "Who? Lori-who? There be no one by that name here, good sir! No, my name is Bagby Butterbottom! That is my name now!"

Erasmus Twiddle thinks sometimes it is a lot of trouble to have a friend. But what can he do? Andrew . . . I mean, Lorimar . . . I mean, Bagby Butterbottom is his friend and that's all there is to it. He cannot get rid of his friends whenever he feels like it. It would not be very friendly.

"We should hurry," says Erasmus. "I don't want to be late for school. A not-detective must never be late for anything. It's unprofessional."

Bagby Butterbottom clears his throat as if he is about to give a long, important speech, but Erasmus tugs him by the arm and they hurry off to school—where, perhaps, the rubber chicken thief is right this minute flopping Mr. Jax's rubber chicken with evil glee.

3

Erasmus Twiddle and Bagby Butterbottom are not the tiniest bit late to school, and as you can see, no one is flopping Mr. Jax's rubber chicken with evil glee. The bell rings, our hero and his friend are already sitting in their seats, and here comes Mrs. Mumuschnitzel, the teacher.

"Good morning, everybody," says Mrs. Mumuschnitzel. "As you all know, today is Show-and-Tell. Who would like to go first? How about Andrew Michaels? Andrew, do you want to go first?"

No one answers because there is no Andrew Michaels in the room. Erasmus whispers something in Mrs. Mumuschnitzel's ear.

"Oh," says Mrs. Mumuschnitzel. "Okay, let me see . . . Bagby? Bagby Butterbottom, how would you like to go first today?"

Bagby is on his feet in a moment. "Hark ye, gentle lady of the lagoons, moons, and other things oons! I would be most happy to oblige," booms he. "Forsooth, I will speaketh a few lines from the most famous play in all the worldeth. Wherefore! Alas! It is called *Hamlet's Pumpernickel Loaf.*"

"I have never heard of such a play," says Mrs. Mumuschnitzel.

But Bagby Butterbottom does not hear the kindly Mrs. Mumuschnitzel. He is already in front of the class speaking in that loud booming voice of his. It is his best actor's voice.

"'To eat or not to eat,'" booms Bagby Butterbottom, "'that is the question! And a silly question it is, because of course I will eat! I will eat most when I am hungry and least when I am not! And when I eat I shall eat this loaf of pumpernickel!' Thank you."

Bagby Butterbottom takes a bow and everyone claps heartily for his fine performance. You can see how much everyone likes Bagby Butterbottom.

"I must find that play in the library so that we can all read it together," says Mrs. Mumuschnitzel. "Now who would like to go next? How about you, Erasmus Twiddle?"

As brave as our brave not-detective is, it makes him nervous to speak in front of so many people. He wishes it did not make him nervous, but it does and there is little he can do about it. Well, he can try not to look nervous and he can tell himself that he will only be talking to people he has talked to lots of times and really there is nothing to be nervous about. This is exactly what he does and—why, here is Erasmus now, looking perfectly calm, standing in front of the entire class.

"I have been working on a most curious mystery," says our hero. "The long and short of it is that Mr. Jax's rubber chicken has been stolen."

It is very, very quiet in the classroom. Everyone is shocked and surprised. Bagby does his best to look as shocked and surprised as everybody else, pretending that this is the first he has heard of the stolen rubber chicken.

"But who would want to steal a rubber chicken?" asks Mrs. Mumuschnitzel. Indeed, it is exactly what everyone is wondering. Erasmus is certainly wondering it. Who on earth or in the sky would want to steal a rubber chicken?

"The good news," says our famous and talented not-detective, "is that no one here is the thief. The thief would not have been as surprised as all of you were."

"Well," says Mrs. Mumuschnitzel, "that's a terrible tragedy for Mr. Jax, but we cannot sit about all day thinking of rubber chickens. Who would like to go next for Show-and-Tell? Anyone?"

No one raises a hand because they are all busy whispering about Mr. Jax's stolen rubber chicken. And that is how it goes the rest of the day at school: No work gets done, none at all, because everyone is talking and whispering about Mr. Jax's stolen rubber chicken. News of the stolen rubber chicken spreads through all of Grmkville, but no one can believe it. No one can believe that someone would steal such a thing. But, of course, they have to believe it because it is so.

"Good riddance!" snarls Henrietta Humphreys. "I should give the thief a reward for having rid Grmkville of that ridiculous rubber beast! But you see how troubled times are, when even the thieves don't know what they're doing! Why, a thief can't buy anything with a rubber chicken! Can you imagine anyone trying to purchase a necklace with a rubber chicken? If that thief had any brains, he would have stolen my money! I am very offended!"

"I never would have thought it," says Sam the Sidewalk Sweeper. "Mr. Jax used to leave his chicken on the sidewalk sometimes when he went into the grocery store. Every now and then people stepped on it and felt a squishy-squish under their feet, but no one ever stole it. I don't understand any of this, but I feel bad for Mr. Jax."

"We don't believe it! Why would anyone want to steal a rubber chicken?" ask Abel and Barry and Cindy and Darryl and Evelyn and Farrell and George and Harold and Izzy and Jared and Kevin and Larry and Mo and Nancy and Ollie and Perry and Quinn and Randy and Susan and Terry and Ursula and Valerie and William and Xavier and Yolanda and Zachary.

Sam the Sidewalk Sweeper is not the only one who feels bad for Mr. Jax. Dotty Polka and Erasmus Twiddle's mother, Mrs. Twiddle, feel bad for him too. They bring him homemade cakes and puddings and pies to try and make him feel better. They even talk of buying Mr. Jax another rubber chicken.

"But I don't want another rubber chicken," says Mr. Jax. "I want *my* rubber chicken back."

Mr. Jax pouts and makes sad faces, but he is never too sad to welcome another cake or pudding into his house.

"Alas and woe! Maybe it would helpeth if you pretended to be a rubber chicken!" booms Bagby Butterbottom, who is on the school playground with our hero, Erasmus Twiddle. "You know, where wouldeth you be if you were a rubber chicken, who would stealeth you, that sort of thing."

Erasmus does not think pretending to be a rubber chicken is a good idea.

"All right, then," says Bagby. "*I* will pretendeth to be a rubber chicken. I will *act!*" And with that, Bagby Butterbottom lies facedown in the grass.

"Nmmmg ym, nmmmg ym," says Bagby. It is hard to understand him because his face is mushed into the grass. He lifts his head. "Nothing yet," he says. "No, I still don't know who would stealeth me. Maybe you should flop me."

But Erasmus does not flop him. Erasmus is busy thinking.

"I am a rubber chicken," urges Bagby. "You have to flop me."

Erasmus is thinking that perhaps the rubber chicken is more valuable than anyone in Grmkville suspects. Yes, this must be so, if someone went to all that trouble to steal it. Perhaps the best way to find out the value of a rubber chicken is to visit the people who made it.

"Exactly what I was thinking," says Erasmus Twiddle.

Luckily for our hero, there is a rubber chicken factory just outside of Grmkville. So off he goes to visit the rubber chicken factory, leaving Bagby Butterbottom with his face in the grass, waiting to be flopped.

Two things could happen at the rubber chicken factory: something very important or nothing of any importance whatsoever. I wonder which it will be.

4

The rubber chicken factory is a big, noisy place where hundreds of rubber chickens are made every minute of every day.

"I have come to find out what makes a rubber chicken valuable," Erasmus tells Woober Willoughby, the owner of the factory.

"Valuable?" says Woober Willoughby.

"Yes," says Erasmus. "What makes a rubber chicken worth stealing?"

Woober Willoughby thinks for a minute. "I don't know why anyone would steal a rubber chicken when we have plenty for sale at reasonable prices," he says sadly. "You ask why rubber chickens are valuable and I must confess, I wish I knew. Business has been terrible. No one is buying rubber chickens anymore. We have a warehouse full of them and we can't sell a

21

single one. We have been thinking of snappy advertisements to try and convince people that they must own a rubber chicken."

"Advertisements?" asks Erasmus.

"Yes, you know, you see them on TV. Tell me what you think of these: Rubber Chickens—A Man's Second Best Friend! Rubber Chickens: They Just Make Sense! New and Improved! 10% More Rubber in Every Chicken! Our Chickens Are Rubberier Than Ever! Why Buy a Regular Chicken When a Rubber Chicken Lasts Forever?"

"Hmm. They're all very good," says Erasmus politely. "It's difficult to choose."

"I know," says Woober. "That's the problem we're having. You should visit Professor Piffle. After all, he invented the rubber chicken. If anyone can help you, Professor Piffle can."

"You mean that Professor Piffle is the person who first put rubber and chicken together?" asks Erasmus.

"That's exactly who he is," says Woober Willoughby.

So off Erasmus goes to visit Professor Piffle. On his way to the Professor's house, he finds Bagby Butterbottom still lying facedown in the grass of the school playground, waiting to be flopped.

"Mm pmmmmmmmm, ymm smm?" says Bagby.

"Bagby," says Erasmus, "you must take your face out of the grass so that I can understand you."

Bagby lifts his face out of the grass. "A professor, you say?" he booms. "I would be only too gladeth to accompany you, good Twiddle!"

So off Erasmus and Bagby go to visit the Professor.

"Ah, the rubber chicken," says Professor Piffle, who is constructing a large contraption of broomsticks and dustbins and string in his living room. "Well, I did invent that, yes, but if you must know, I was trying to make a rubber rooster."

"But why would a person want to steal a rubber chicken?" asks Erasmus.

"Steal a rubber chicken?" says the Professor. "I don't know. It can't do anything and isn't worth very much money. Would you like to see my many awards and degrees from all the best schools in the world?"

Erasmus is about to answer this question when Bagby—who is a very curious fellow—presses a button on the Professor's contraption and a marble shoots out of it and breaks a window.

"That wasn't supposed to happen," says Professor Piffle.

"I would like to take a closer look at that window, if I may," says Erasmus.

And take a closer look at the window he does. There is a large hole in the center of it and bits of glass on the carpet and many more bits on the ground outside.

"Hmm," whispers Erasmus, "very curious. "Professor, thank you for your time, but I think we must be going now."

Outside of the Professor's house, Bagby turns to his friend with a very serious frown. "Why, good and honorable Twiddle, why dideth we leave the house of yonder Professor so quickly?"

"Bagby," says our famous and talented not-detective, "I have solved this case. It's time we paid a visit to Mr. Jax."

5

Mr. Jax sits in his room of doodads, surrounded not only by his doodads, but also by cakes and puddings. He has eaten a great deal of cake and pudding and has a bit of pudding on his nose.

"Mr. Jax," says Erasmus Twiddle. "I know who stole your rubber chicken."

"Do you?" asks Mr. Jax, suddenly nervous.

"Yes," continues Erasmus, "You see, if a person—a thief, say—were to break a window from the *outside*, then most of the broken glass would fall on the *inside*. And if he were to break a window from the *inside*, then most of the broken glass would fall on the *outside*."

"Yes, well, ahem," says Mr. Jax, who fidgets as if he has to go to the bathroom.

"Now if you look at the window that was broken by your thief," continues Erasmus, "you will see that the bits of broken glass have fallen mostly on the outside, not the inside."

Both Bagby and Mr. Jax look at the broken window. It is exactly as Erasmus says it is—most of the broken glass is on the outside.

24

"Begads!" booms Bagby. "Wherefore! The right, honorable Twiddle is correcteth!"

"This means," Erasmus tells Mr. Jax, "that the thief was inside your house when he broke the window. Why would a thief break the window if he was already inside the house?"

"Well, er, yes, that is a very interesting question," says Mr. Jax. "But I'm afraid I forgot about a meeting I'm supposed to attend—the Collectors Association of Collecting Collectibles, you know."

"Really, the thief had no reason to break the window at all and—"

"I didn't do it!" cries Mr. Jax suddenly, throwing up his arms and—what's this?—out of the baggy left sleeve of his jacket flies his rubber chicken. It flops against the ceiling and then flops to the ground, where it sits looking floppy and useless as only a rubber chicken can.

Mr. Jax smiles and whistles and tries to act as if nothing is at all out of the ordinary, but it is no use. Our famous and talented not-detective has caught him.

"You are very clever, Erasmus," says Mr. Jax finally. "Yes, I broke the window myself and pretended that someone stole my rubber chicken."

"Dear sir!" booms Bagby Butterbottom, who has helped himself to a little butterscotch pudding. "Heretofore! Woe! That is not at all honorable! Why dideth you do such a thing? Alas! This is very fine pudding, by the way."

"My rubber chicken makes me happy," says Mr. Jax, "and I was tired of people thinking it was a silly, worthless thing. How would they like it if I thought what they cared about was silly and worthless? I don't think they would like it in the least."

Erasmus does not think they would like it either. Erasmus himself certainly would not like it. He would not like it if someone thought that solving mysteries were a silly thing.

"I hoped people might see that my rubber chicken wasn't silly and worthless if someone went to the trouble of stealing it," says Mr. Jax. "And that is exactly what happened."

"Oof, that is a lot to thinketh about," says Bagby Butterbottom. "I ate too much pudding and am very sleepy. I hope you don't mind if I take a nap." And with that, Bagby promptly falls asleep on the floor, where he uses the rubber chicken as a pillow, proving that a rubber chicken is not quite as useless as we all thought.

"I don't think you can steal something from yourself," says Erasmus Twiddle. "And since there has been no crime, or only a very little one, there will be no punishment."

"I'm glad," says Mr. Jax. "I don't like punishments."

"It is true," continues Erasmus, "that I spent a lot of time on this case because I thought there'd been a crime. But no time is wasted that is spent . . . that is . . . well, that is spent trying to find a stolen rubber chicken, whether the rubber chicken is actually stolen or not. A missing rubber chicken is still a mystery. But this case has been solved and I should be going. You will take excellent care of my friend, Bagby Butterbottom, until he wakes?"

"I will," says Mr. Jax.

Very well, then. Our hero leaves Mr. Jax's house, but not

before he takes a cupcake to eat as he makes his way home.

"Nothing that makes a person happy can be silly and worthless," concludes Erasmus Twiddle. "It doesn't matter if it's solving a mystery—as it is with me—or acting—as it is with Bagby—or whether it's a bag of rocks, an old boot, a beachball, a lump of cheese, a contraption made of broomsticks and dustbins and string, a bowl of butterscotch pudding or a rubber chicken."

Very wise words, Erasmus Twiddle. Very wise words, indeed.

the Beginning of a Most Mysterious Mystery

Being a not-detective is a lot like being a tuba player except that a not-detective does not necessarily know how to play a tuba. A tuba player, you see, is always a tuba player whether or not he happens to be playing his tuba. Similarly, a not-detective is always a not-detective whether or not he happens to be recovering a stolen rubber chicken. So Erasmus Twiddle is never just Erasmus Twiddle. He is always Erasmus Twiddle, the famous and talented not-detective (he is never ever Erasmus Twiddle, the tuba player). Which is just a unique way of saying

that here is Erasmus now, strolling along the Grmkville streets, minding his not-detective business.

"I don't know," says Erasmus Twiddle. "Yes, I understand, but it sounds kind of dangerous."

Who is our hero talking to? He is all alone so I guess he's talking to himself. It is not the best thing in the world for a famous and talented not-detective to talk to himself in public like this. It looks, well, not quite right. Sometimes talking to yourself in public is okay. If there is something important that you need to tell yourself so you don't forget, well, you should probably go ahead and tell yourself this important thing. Or if you see something funny like an enraged elephant with a tiny head and you want to make yourself laugh, you should probably go ahead and tell yourself about the enraged elephant with a tiny head. But a famous and talented not-detective is different from you and me. He has a reputation to protect. If he goes around talking to himself too much, people might think he's weird.

"No . . . uh huh . . . uh huh . . . too dangerous, yes," says Erasmus Twiddle.

Wait a minute. Our hero is not talking to himself. Look closely and you will see something flying loopty-loops next to his ear. Whatever it is, it is not even an inch long. Why, it's a bug!

"Of course it's too dangerous," squeaks the bug. "That's why I have to do it. What kind of daredevil would I be if I only did safe, easy stunts like skip three times while touching my elbows and singing the national anthem? Being a weevil, I don't have elbows, but you know I mean."

Perhaps you are wondering what a weevil is. Well, a weevil is a kind of beetle. It is a snout beetle, to be precise. What is a snout beetle? Well, imagine a beetle. Okay, now imagine a beetle with a pig's nose. That's a weevil.

"I said I would do it and I'll do it! I'll cycle through eleven apples on my weevilcycle or my name isn't Weevil Kneevil!" squeaks Weevil Kneevil, the bug, as he lands on our hero's

29

shoulder. "Look, no wings!" And with that, the daredevil weevil hops off Erasmus's shoulder and falls promptly to the ground.

"Very impressive," says Erasmus, who does not think it so impressive for a bug to fall to the ground without using his wings.

Erasmus is careful not to step on Weevil Kneevil and Weevil Kneevil picks himself up and once again flies daring loopty-loops next to our hero's ear. Before long, they come to Erasmus's house, where they find a letter on the doorstep. I do not mean a letter "B" or "F" or anything like that. I mean a letter of the kind you might receive in the mail from someone far away.

"But there's no stamp on this letter," says a thoughtful Erasmus Twiddle. "It's just a folded piece of paper and it's hardly even wrinkled. Because of these things, I don't think this letter came through the mail and I don't think it came from far away. Someone right here in Grmkville who is not a mailman must have put this letter on my doorstep."

You see why Erasmus is the not-detective and not me. Anyway, what our hero holds in his hand is not really a letter. It is a poem:

Erasmus Twiddle thinks he's clever,
  Villains and thieves outsmart him never.
Isn't he great, folks? I say, Pooh!
  Let evil reign, that's what I'll do.

Wherever I go, trouble will follow.
  Every furgle and fleb and grumber and hojie,

Every ploff and yonk and oogoo and eebee,
  Villainous villain that I am, I'll take them all—ho!
I'll prove Twiddle's not cleverer than a shoe.
  Let's see if he can catch me. This poem's his clue!

Erasmus stands there, reading and rereading the poem and wondering who could have sent it to him.

"I am also wondering what a furgle, fleb, grumber, hojie, ploff, yonk, oogoo, and eebee are," says our hero.

"For my next stunt, I will fly twenty-seven backflips with my eyes closed or my name isn't Weevil Kneevil!" squeaks Weevil Kneevil. And the little weevil starts flying his backflips.

Weevil Kneevil is so busy concentrating that he does not hear the loud screech of a car as it stops in front of Erasmus Twiddle's house. Nor does the backflipping Weevil Kneevil notice Travis Plunkett hop out of the car and run up to our hero, cupping his hands in front of him.

"Look!" cries Travis Plunkett. "Look, look at my furgle!" He holds up his hands but they are empty.

"I don't see any furgle," says Erasmus Twiddle, who wouldn't know a furgle if he saw one.

"Exactly," says Travis Plunkett. "My furgle has disappeared. I put it in my pants, which I do every Tuesday at one o'clock, and when I jiggled my legs two hours later it was gone."

"Hmm," says Erasmus Twiddle. He studies the mysterious poem that was left on his doorstep. *Every furgle and fleb and grumber and hojie, every ploff and yonk and oogoo and eebee. Villainous villian that I am, I'll take them all—ho!*

31

"I know who has your furgle," Erasmus tells Travis Plunkett.

"You do?" says Travis. "That was fast, even for a famous and talented not-detective. Who has my furgle?"

"Whoever wrote this poem," answers Erasmus.

This is not the kind of answer Travis Plunkett was expecting. He has never heard of Whoever Wrote This Poem.

"Twenty-seven!" squeaks Weevil Kneevil, who finishes his backflips and settles on our hero's shoulder to rest. He is a dizzy Weevil Kneevil.

"Tell me," Erasmus says to Travis Plunkett, "what is a furgle?"

"You've never heard of a furgle?" exclaims Travis Plunkett in disbelief. "Who's never heard of a furgle? A furgle is . . . " Travis makes a bunch of strange hand gestures, ". . . and it's sort of . . ." Travis makes another bunch of strange hand gestures, ". . . and *that's* what a furgle is. My furgle is the most important thing in my life. I am nothing without my furgle. I really must get it back by Friday. I'm having some people over and we're going to play Twister."

"I see," says Erasmus, who would probably understand why a furgle is so important, why Travis puts it in his pants every Tuesday at one o'clock, or what it has to do with the game Twister, if he only knew what a furgle was.

Erasmus points at Travis's pants. "Are those the pants you were wearing when your furgle disappeared?"

"No, these are those pants," answers Travis Plunkett, and holds up a pair of blue jeans.

"I would like to examine them, if I may," says our hero.

Erasmus turns the pockets of the jeans inside out but finds nothing. Being a thorough not-detective, he must conduct a thorough examination, so he shoves his left arm into the right leg of the jeans and he shoves his right arm into the left leg of the jeans and he puts his head in the seat of the pants so that he cannot see anything. Weevil Kneevil—who, you may remember, was resting on our hero's shoulder—is stuck in the pants and buzzing around trying to get out.

"I don't see anything unusual," mumbles Erasmus from inside the pants. "Travis, why don't you show me how you jiggled?"

Travis jiggles. The thing is, Erasmus cannot see him, what with his head in Travis's pants. Our hero looks a little funny wearing pants on his head. This is not the best time for our hero to look funny. After all, according to the mysterious poem left on his doorstep, a fleb will be stolen next, and then a grumber, hojie, ploff, yonk, oogoo, and eebee. If these things are as important to their owners as a furgle is to Travis Plunkett . . . well, Erasmus should do something. He should not stand around with pants on his head.

What's that? Do you hear? The sound of footsteps hurrying toward our hero. Is it a friend? Is it the victim of a crime coming for help? Or is it the furgle thief making a sneak attack on Erasmus Twiddle? I guess you will just have to read "The Case of the Lonely Rabbit-Hippo" before you find out. By no means should you skip ahead to discover what happens next in this most mysterious mystery. Thank you.

the case
of the
Lonely Rabbit-Hippo

1

There are many creatures
in this world—creatures that
walk and creatures that run,
creatures that crawl and creatures
that gallop, creatures that swim, fly
and slither, creatures that hop, skip
and jump, not to mention
creatures that gambol,
lope, canter, scuttle,
dig, burrow, and
swing from
tree to
tree. And
whichever
of these a
creature

does, it always seems to be just exactly what that creature should be doing. You do not see a galloping fish because a galloping fish would be all wrong. You do not see a scuttling elephant because a scuttling elephant would be all wrong. And perhaps a slithering monkey or a caterpillar that swings from tree to tree would be the most wrong of all. But a crawling giraffe does not sound all that good either.

Anyway, it is not unusual that the people of Grmkville are frightened when a big, strange, hopping creature hops into town, making all kinds of louder than loud noise and shaking anything and everything with its hopping. They have never before seen anything like this creature and it is really much too big to be hopping. It does not seem at all right that such a big creature hops. But hop it does, and it is quite good at it. Boom boom b o o m ! Boom boom boom! That is the thunderous sound of the creature's hopping.

"Excuse me," says the big, strange,

hopping creature to Mrs. Frumplebee. But Mrs. Frumplebee does not at all enjoy finding herself so close to this big, hopping thing and runs off.

"Excuse me," says the creature to Mr. Jax, who darts past with his beloved rubber chicken flopping in his hand. "You'll never get my rubber chicken, you big, strange, hopping creature!" yells Mr. Jax.

It must be admitted that the people of Grmkville are not being very polite. Usually, they are no more or less polite than people should be—which only means that if you, a total stranger, were to walk into Grmkville, they would most certainly be polite to you. They would be polite to you even if you *hopped* into Grmkville. But then you are smaller than this creature and do not make such a terrible noise, nor shake and rattle so many things, with your hopping.

"Excuse me," says the creature to Paramus Plotz. "Pardon," says the creature to Suzy Loopy. "Pardonnez-moi," says the creature to a particularly French-looking Grmkvillian who is not at all French and whose name happens to be Bill.

But Paramus Plotz, Suzy Loopy, and Bill (who is not at all French) are much too frightened to stop and chat with this big, strange, hopping creature, so they run away.

"I only want to know where I can find the famous not-detective, Erasmus Twiddle," says the creature. But no one is listening because the lonely creature is alone, as lonely creatures often are.

So, with a ho and a hum, the big, strange, hopping creature hops down one street, then another. Boom boom

boom! **Boom boom boom!** People peek at him from behind the shutters of their shaking and rattling houses. **Boom boom boom! Boom boom boom!** The creature has done quite a lot of hopping today and he is getting tired. Perhaps he will never find Erasmus Twiddle. It certainly seems as though he will never find Erasmus Twiddle. He is about to give up his search when—what's this? Why, it's a nifty little house with a sign in the front yard:

ERASMUS TWIDDLE—THE FAMOUS NOT-DETECTIVE
PLEASE DON'T CALL HIM A DETECTIVE BECAUSE ANYBODY
CAN BE A DETECTIVE AND HE'S JUST A BOY WHO LIKES TO SOLVE
MYSTERIES AND HAPPENS TO BE GOOD AT SOLVING MYSTERIES, BUT BECAUSE
IT'S SO EASY TO BECOME A DETECTIVE AND ALL YOU HAVE TO DO IS SEND FOUR BOTTLE CAPS, THREE
PROOF-OF-PURCHASE SEALS FROM YOUR FAVORITE CEREAL, TWO AA BATTERIES, AND ONE RATTLESNAKE SKIN TO P.O. BOX 12345

The creature cannot possibly read this entire sign; having to puzzle over so many words would make him dizzy. Besides, he forgot his glasses and it is impossible for him to read all those tiny words.

"But why do I need to read all those tiny words?" asks the creature. "I can read enough to see that I have found Erasmus Twiddle!"

This is very true. And while the rest of us might walk up and knock on the front door, the big, strange, hopping creature does no such thing. Instead, he stays right where he is and hops up and down, up and down to get the attention of you know who—by which I mean our famous and talented not-detective, Erasmus Twiddle.

2

Boom boom boom! **Boom boom boom!** The whole block shakes and rattles, and Erasmus Twiddle, who is having lunch with his mother, watches his sandwich bounce off the table and onto the floor.

"Whoopsy," says Erasmus Twiddle's mother. "My, my."

"I suppose that large, odder than odd creature sitting in the front yard is here to see me," says Erasmus Twiddle. "I have never seen anything like it before, but I'm not scared. Not-detectives don't get scared. It would be unprofessional. I guess I'll go outside and see what it wants."

Perhaps Erasmus really isn't scared, as he says. Or perhaps he isn't—that is to say, perhaps he isn't *not* scared, which is only another way of saying that perhaps he is scared. Yes, he might be a tiny bit scared and just pretends that he isn't because the neighbors are watching him from across the street.

"What is it? What does it want? Will it eat us? Why won't it go away?" cry the neighbors.

"I am the lonely rabbit-hippo," the creature says to Erasmus Twiddle.

Indeed, now that the crea-ture mentions it, he does look like a

38

rabbit-hippo. He is the size and shape of a hippo. Yes, he is exactly like a hippo in every way except that he has rabbit ears and the hind legs of a rabbit.

"Were you the one making all that noise?" asks our hero.

"Oh, mercy me," replies the rabbit-hippo, "I might have been. The life of a rabbit-hippo is so full of confusing things. I was only hopping. I'll show you how I hop if you promise not to run away."

"I promise not to run away," says Erasmus Twiddle.

"No. You must put a finger in your ear, stand on one leg, and say, 'Fuddlepuddle oh fuddlepuddle, by the powers vested in me by nada and nobody, I promise I will not run away.' That is a proper promise."

Erasmus Twiddle thinks this is silly, but as he is not familiar with the customs of rabbit-hippos and it is probably the custom of rabbit-hippos to make promises in this way, he does as the creature asks. He puts a finger in his ear and stands on one leg.

"Fuddlepuddle oh fuddlepuddle," says Erasmus Twiddle, "by the powers vested in me by nada and nobody, I promise I will not run away."

No sooner does our famous and talented not-detective utter these words then the rabbit-hippo, with a big kick of his back feet, starts hopping around the lawn. Boom boom boom! **Boom boom boom!** Windows rattle and trees shiver. Boom boom boom! **Boom boom boom!** Cars bounce and houses shake.

Boom boom boom! **Boom boom boo—**

"Stop! Enough!" cries Erasmus Twiddle, who has fallen to the ground because of all this booming. "Please stop!"

The rabbit-hippo sits on the front lawn, whistling.

"It was definitely you making all that noise," says our famous and talented not-detective.

"Well," replies the rabbit-hippo, "I do apologize. But I am only doing what rabbit-hippos do. I am hopping to and fro and all about."

Where do rabbit-hippos come from? Erasmus Twiddle has not learned about them in school. He has never seen one in a zoo. This rabbit-hippo must have come from very far away to see our famous and talented not-detective. Which indeed he has. He has come from The Land of Rabbit-Hippos.

"You are the famous not-detective, Erasmus Twiddle, are you not?" asks the rabbit-hippo.

"I am," says Erasmus, a little proudly.

"That is good because, well, you see, I have not one friend in the world. I am a nice rabbit-hippo—you will not meet a nicer one—and I would be very thoughtful to my friends if I had any. But—"

"You must have one friend," interrupts Erasmus Twiddle. It is not polite to interrupt, but Erasmus could not help himself. How could the creature not have a single friend in the world?

"No, I do not," replies the rabbit-hippo. "I will show you what happens when I try to make a friend."

He turns his big hippo head with its bunny ears toward the neighbors. With a kick of his back feet, he hops toward them, crushing shrubs and footballs and bicycles along the way. The rabbit-hippo does not mean to crush these things. It is just that he cannot see very well when he's hopping.

Frightened, the neighbors try to run away, but the ground shakes so much that they stumble and fall about. It is clear that the rabbit-hippo is not going to make any friends here and the lonely creature hops back to Erasmus Twiddle.

"Tell me," says Erasmus, "you've really heard about me in a land as far away as The Land of Rabbit-Hippos?"

"Oh yes," says the lonely rabbit-hippo. "You are very famous in The Land of Rabbit-Hippos. Will you help me find a friend?"

"Hmm," says Erasmus. "I am famous for solving mysteries. This is certainly not a mystery. You don't have any friends because you scare people with all of your hopping. But I suppose figuring out how to make people not afraid of you and want to be your friend—well, that is a mystery. Besides, I am not one to turn away from any creature in need of help, especially a lonely creature. I will help you."

"Hippo hippo hooray!" cries the rabbit-hippo, who is so happy that he becomes quite hoppy and hops all over the lawn, crushing flowers and plants and a skateboard and anything that is unlucky enough to be underfoot.

3

After many minutes of happy hopping, the rabbit-hippo rests quietly on the lawn, catching his breath.

"First," Erasmus Twiddle tells him, "I will take you to see Mrs. Ploppityplop. She isn't afraid of a little loud hopping and she is one of the nicest people in all of Grmkville. I'm sure she will be your friend."

"And I will be Mrs. Ploppityplop's friend!" says the hopeful rabbit-hippo. He starts to sing a little song, which goes like this:

"Mrs. Ploppityplop, I like her a lot.
Mrs. Ploppityplop, she has a big pot.
But she can't cook me, 'cause . . .
'Cause I'm too big to fit in a pot . . .
And I like her a lot and, uh . . .
. . . blot."

The rabbit-hippo is not much good at making up songs. It is time that he and Erasmus were off to Mrs. Ploppityplop's anyway.

"I am only a rabbit-hippo," says the rabbit-hippo, "and I don't know much, but I think it would be easier if you rode on my back."

"Yes, I suppose so," says Erasmus Twiddle.

Our famous and talented not-detective climbs onto the rabbit-hippo's back.

"I would just like to say," announces Erasmus Twiddle, "that I am not at all afraid to ride on the back of a hopping rabbit-hippo, no matter how dangerous it might be, because, of course, not-detectives are not afraid of a little hopping."

"That is all well and good," says the rabbit-hippo, "but you'd better hold on to my ears."

Erasmus holds on to the creature's ears, and off the two of

them go, hopping to Mrs. Ploppityplop's house. The rabbit-hippo hops as if nothing at all is out of the ordinary, crushing basketballs, plants, golf clubs, seesaws, wheelbarrows, park benches, and shovels along the way. "Uh oh!" says Erasmus. "Look out!" says Erasmus. But what our hero says most of all is "Oops!" because if he happens to yell something like, "Watch out for that nice, new, inflatable water buffalo!" the rabbit-hippo is sure to hop right on top of the nice, new, inflatable water buffalo and that is the end of the water buffalo, if you know what I mean.

Yes, it is quite a sight to see Erasmus Twiddle riding on the back of this lonely rabbit-hippo. And wherever Erasmus and the rabbit-hippo hop, the people of Grmkville run away. The Grmkvillians should not be scared of the rabbit-hippo. He is a well-meaning creature, even if he is very large and his hopping makes a louder than loud noise and he crushes a few things. The Grmkvillians should not be scared, but that does not mean that they won't be.

"I'm not scared!" sneers Henrietta Humphreys, the richest and roundest lady in all of Grmkville. "I have a very big alarm system that will keep a hippo-rabbit-thing or any other unwelcome beast out of my house! That silly hippo-rabbit-thing would not scare other silly hippo-rabbit-things with all of its hopping! Why doesn't it go home and make friends there? Why does it need to make friends with *us*?"

"It isn't so much the hopping that scares me," says Sam the Sidewalk Sweeper. "It's the pooping. That's a very big animal, so he must make very big poop. I would hate to see such big poop on my sidewalks. Someone could drown in it. Besides, it is not in my job description to clean up poop. My job description states very clearly that poop of any size is to be cleaned up by the pooper or a member of the pooper's party. But that big pooper doesn't have a party and, well, I just hope he doesn't poop on the sidewalk, because I know I'll get stuck cleaning it up and it will take days and days."

"A rabbit-hippo! Aaaaaarrrgh!" cry Abel and Barry and Cindy and Darryl and Evelyn and Farrell and George and Harold and Izzy and Jared and Kevin and Larry and Mo and Nancy and Ollie and Perry and Quinn and Randy and Susan and Terry and Ursula and Valerie and William and Xavier and Yolanda and Zachary.

Erasmus Twiddle and the lonely rabbit-hippo have now arrived in front of Mrs. Ploppityplop's house.

"Where is my friend, Mrs. Ploppityplop?" asks the rabbit-hippo, turning his big hippo head with its bunny ears this way and that.

"Now listen, rabbit-hippo," says our famous and talented not-detective, "Mrs. Ploppityplop is not an old lady but she lost all her teeth in an accident with a garden hose. She has a set of false teeth that she pops in and out of her mouth. The teeth look a little funny. Just pretend you don't notice."

"Okey-dokey," says the rabbit-hippo. "But where is Mrs. Ploppityplop? I don't see her anywhere."

"Here I am," says Mrs. Ploppityplop, through her closed front door. She has locked herself inside her house, which is not a very friendly way to greet a rabbit-hippo. "I heard the terrible noise that animal made!" says Mrs. Ploppityplop through her closed door. "Boom! boom! boom! Any animal that makes so much noise is not a nice animal! It knocked my teeth out of my head and now I can't find them! I don't have anything to say to that not-nice animal!"

"You're talking very well for someone without teeth," says the rabbit-hippo.

Erasmus elbows the rabbit-hippo, which means *Don't say anything about Mrs. Ploppityplop's teeth!*

"Mrs. Ploppityplop," says Erasmus, "I will find your teeth for you if you promise to come out and say hello to the rabbit-hippo."

There is a long silence, then: "Only if you find *my* teeth," says Mrs. Ploppityplop, "and not somebody else's. I once put somebody else's teeth in my mouth by mistake and it was awful."

Erasmus agrees and, luckily, nobody else has lost a set of teeth near Mrs. Ploppityplop's house. Our hero searches around the house and, being as good a not-detective as he is, quickly finds Mrs. Ploppityplop's teeth in a bush.

"Slip them through the mail slot," Mrs. Ploppityplop tells him.

Erasmus does as he is instructed, and after a minute the front door creaks open and out pops Mrs. Ploppityplop's head.

"I'll only do it if that rabbit-hippo takes two hops back," says Mrs. Ploppityplop. "I don't want him so close to me."

The rabbit-hippo—who is very excited because he is about to make a friend—takes two little hops back. Mrs. Ploppityplop comes out of her house.

"Hello, rabbit-hippo," says Mrs. Ploppityplop.

"Hallo, Mrs. Ploppityplop!" cries the rabbit-hippo, who is so pleased that he takes one single, gigantic hop forward and lands right on Mrs. Ploppityplop's big toe.

"Ow! Ow! Ow!" says Mrs. Ploppityplop, hopping on one foot in terrible pain.

Perhaps the rabbit-hippo thinks Mrs. Ploppityplop's hopping is some kind of new-friend dance, because he takes one look at that hopping lady and *he* begins hopping right along with her. Boom boom boom! **Boom boom boom!** Erasmus and Mrs. Ploppityplop fall to the ground. The excited rabbit-hippo stops hopping and waits to see what he and his new friend will do next.

But Mrs. Ploppityplop is not so friendly anymore. In fact, she is not friendly at all. She opens her mouth to say something mean to the rabbit-hippo. "You beastly—" she says. But then her teeth, which have been rattled loose by all the rabbit-hippo's hopping, fall out of her mouth and right into the bush where Erasmus found them.

"Ouf!" huffs a toothless, swollen-toed Mrs. Ploppityplop. She limps straight back into her house and locks the door.

"If Mrs. Ploppityplop is one of the nicest people in Grmkville," says a confused rabbit-hippo, "then I think I'm in trouble."

46

"Certainly you saw what you did to Mrs. Ploppityplop's toe?" asks Erasmus.

"Actually, no," replies the rabbit-hippo. "I can't see very well when I hop."

Erasmus thinks for a minute. "You know, rabbit-hippo, you are very large and because of this it is very upsetting when you hop. So if we're going to find you a friend, you'll have to not hop. Let's get away from Mrs. Ploppityplop's house."

This really confuses the rabbit-hippo, because if he cannot hop then he cannot get away from Mrs. Ploppityplop's house.

"Are you going to carry me?" the creature asks.

"Of course not," says Erasmus. He climbs onto the rabbit-hippo's back. "*Now* you must hop. *Later* you must not. Hop to that field over there, please."

The rabbit-hippo gives a big kick of his back feet and . . . boom boom boom, **boom boom boom** . . . hops over to the field.

"Now you sit in this field," Erasmus tells the rabbit-hippo, "and I'll bring No One in Particular here to meet you. She's one of the friendliest people in all of Grmkville and I am sure she'll be your friend."

"And I will be friends with no one in particular!" cries a hopeful rabbit-hippo. "Only . . . only that doesn't sound too good—being friends with no one in particular, I mean. That doesn't sound any different than—"

"No, you silly rabbit-hippo, you don't understand. No One in Particular is a girl's name. She is very nice. Just don't hop and you'll soon have a friend."

And with that, Erasmus goes off to find No One in Particular. While the rabbit-hippo is waiting, he hums a little song, which goes like this:

"Me and no one in particular,
We'll be best friends-icular,
That's me and no one in particular."

The rabbit-hippo is really quite bad at making up songs. What's taking Erasmus so long? The rabbit-hippo is getting tired of waiting and he has such an urge to hop—just one or two little hops. But no, he'd better not, because here comes Erasmus now, with a girl humming and skipping along beside him.

"Well, here she is," says Erasmus Twiddle. "No One in Particular, please say hello to the gentle rabbit-hippo."

No One in Particular takes one look at the big, strange creature before her—this creature that is the size and shape of a hippo but has the ears and the hind legs of a rabbit—she takes one look and says: "That's not a rabbit-hippo! It's a headless boober!" And that is the last we see of No One in Particular, because she runs off.

"What's a headless boober?" asks Erasmus.

"You're asking the wrong rabbit-hippo," says the rabbit-hippo. "I'm new to this country. But what is most confusing is that she called me 'headless' and I believe that I do, in fact, have a head."

"Yes, rabbit-hippo," comforts Erasmus Twiddle. "You have a head. A big one too, a great big rabbit-hippo head."

48

4

The rabbit-hippo is sadder than he has ever been.

"I don't think I'll ever find a friend," says the big, lonely creature.

"You know," says a thoughtful Erasmus Twiddle, "as a famous and talented not-detective, I must think of a mystery from every which way, and it seems to me that you have already found a friend."

"Where?" says the rabbit-hippo, turning his big hippo head with its bunny ears to the left and to the right. "I don't see anybody."

"I mean me," says Erasmus. "Friends help each other, and I'm helping you, or I'm trying to help you, so that makes me your friend. Besides, it's fun to sit on your back when you hop."

The rabbit-hippo has never thought of any of this before. But he is still suspicious. "You don't even know my favorite color."

"Well, what is your favorite color, rabbit-hippo?"

"Blue."

"Now I know that your favorite color is blue," declares Erasmus Twiddle.

This seems to make the rabbit-hippo pretty happy. He has at last found a friend! He is about to hop for joy when . . . uh oh. Here comes Mrs. Ploppityplop with the swollen toe. She has a large crowd of angry Grmkvillians with her, and they are all carrying nets and look quite mean, which is how people look when they are angry.

49

"Of course we look mean!" snarls Henrietta Humphreys, who is being carried by three of her servants. "We have been put upon by a monstrous beast with monstrous nostrils! It's also very tiring to be carried by your servants in this heat and I'm cranky! What a bother—having to capture some horrendous hippo-rabbit-thing that should know its proper place is with other hippo-rabbit-things and not with us!"

"I don't mean to look mean," says Sam the Sidewalk Sweeper. "I was sweeping a sidewalk like I usually am and this crowd came by and swept me up in it. And instead of my broom, now I have this net. I can't sweep a sidewalk with a net."

"Meanies we be! Meanies we be!" cry Abel and Barry and Cindy and Darryl and Evelyn and Farrell and George and Harold and Izzy and Jared and Kevin and Larry and Mo and Nancy and Ollie and Perry and Quinn and Randy and Susan and Terry and Ursula and Valerie and William and Xavier and Yolanda and Zachary.

"We've come for the rabbit-hippo," says Mrs. Ploppityplop with the swollen toe. "City ordinance number 44444444–4444444–444444444444444444–44–44–0004–0000–000–00–0 states very clearly that no rabbit-hippos shall be kept in Grmkville without written consent from Somebody Very Important. Do you have written consent from Somebody Very Important?"

"I don't think so," answers Erasmus Twiddle.

"Then I hereby demand that you hand over the rabbit-hippo," demands Mrs. Ploppityplop with the swollen toe.

"Hello, Erasmus." Why, it's Mrs. Twiddle, Erasmus

Twiddle's mother, and she is carrying a net just like the rest of the angry Grmkvillians! "I only wanted to bring you your lunch, which you didn't finish," says Mrs. Twiddle. She holds out her net and inside it is our hero's lunchbox.

"Thank you," says Erasmus, taking his lunchbox. "I will eat when I am more at leisure."

"Enough!" says Mrs. Ploppityplop with the swollen toe. "Let's get the rabbit-hippo."

Things look bad for the lonely rabbit-hippo (who, it must be admitted, is not quite as lonely as he used to be since he has made a friend). The angry Grmkvillians raise their nets, about to capture him. As you might imagine, the rabbit-hippo is not very happy about this. So with a big kick of his back feet, he starts hopping to and fro and all about. Boom boom boom! **Boom boom boom!** The angry Grmkvillians become the scared Grmkvillians. They drop their nets and stumble away as fast as they can. The rabbit-hippo hops on the nets, crushing them as much as nets can be crushed. Which isn't very much, really.

"Whoa there, rabbit-hippo," says Erasmus. "I think you can stop now. You've pretty much crushed the nets."

"It seems that by being my friend," says the rabbit-hippo, "you make a lot of enemies."

This certainly appears to be true. It is not fair that people get mad at Erasmus just because he makes friends with a creature they do not like. But then, it might seem unfair to others that Erasmus is friends with a hopping rabbit-hippo.

"Rabbit-hippo," declares Erasmus Twiddle, "I said I'm your

friend and I will stay your friend—although, it isn't good for a not-detective to have a lot of enemies. Let's go see Professor Piffle. He knows a lot of things and maybe he can help us."

So Erasmus once again climbs onto the rabbit-hippo's back, and off they hop to Professor Piffle's house, the rabbit-hippo crushing a tennis ball, a pot, and a—

"Watch out for that tricycle!" yells Erasmus.

But it is too late. The rabbit-hippo crushes the tricycle with one mighty hop and continues Boom boom booming on his way.

5

Erasmus and the rabbit-hippo come hopping up to Professor Piffle's house and find the Professor wearing an inner tube around his waist and bouncing himself against a fence. The ways of a scientist are very mysterious.

The Professor stops his bouncing and studies the rabbit-hippo. "What you have here, young Erasmus," says Professor Piffle, "is a Rabbitpotamus. I quote from *The Big Book of Strange Creatures*: 'The Rabbitpotamus can live to be 103 years old and likes carrots.'"

Professor Piffle pulls a carrot from his pocket.

"Yum," says the rabbit-hippo.

"The Rabbitpotamus also likes beets," says the Professor. He pulls a beet from his pocket.

"Ew," says the rabbit-hippo. "I don't like beets."

"Funny. Neither do I," says Professor Piffle.

"Maybe *you're* a Rabbitpotamus too," suggests the rabbit-hippo.

Professor Piffle thinks about this. As a scientist, he must admit that such a thing is possible. He hops, but it is just a little hop and hardly makes any noise at all. Clearly, he is not a Rabbitpotamus. He's just Professor Piffle.

"I've never seen a real live Rabbitpotamus before," says Professor Piffle. "I wonder, Erasmus, if you wouldn't mind taking a picture of us?"

"I have to make sure my whiskers are straight, if I'm going to be in a picture," says the rabbit-hippo.

This big, strange, hopping creature looks at himself in a mirror and finds that his whiskers are straight and that he is a very handsome rabbit-hippo. The Professor puts his arm around the rabbit-hippo and smiles for the camera. Click!

Perhaps you are thinking that the rabbit-hippo now has not one friend, but two—Erasmus Twiddle and Professor Piffle. If you are thinking this, then pat yourself on the back, because you are very clever. And if you are not thinking this, well, pat yourself on the back anyway, because I'm sure you are still very clever.

Erasmus stares at the inner tube around the Professor's waist. "Inner tube. Tire. Wheel. Wheels. Skates!" says our hero. "We should go now, rabbit-hippo."

"May I join you?" asks Professor Piffle. "I would like to observe the behavior of a Rabbitpotamus . . . if it's okay with the Rabbitpotamus, that is."

"It's okey-dokey with me," says the rabbit-hippo.

53

So Erasmus and Professor Piffle climb onto the rabbit-hippo's back, and after a few very loud hops, they arrive in front of Dotty Polka's Roller Disco.

"Dotty Polka," says Erasmus, "I know you're hiding inside your roller disco because you're afraid of the rabbit-hippo and all of his loud hopping. You're the best roller disco teacher in all of Grmkville—well, um, you're the only roller disco teacher in all of Grmkville. If you teach the rabbit-hippo how to roller disco, then he won't have to hop around. A rabbit-hippo that roller discos is much quieter than a rabbit-hippo that hops. A rabbit-hippo that roller discos wouldn't scare people so much; he would entertain them with his roller disco moves and make many friends."

"I don't have any skates that would fit such a big creature," says Dotty Polka from inside her roller disco.

"Excuse me," says Professor Piffle, "but I'm sure that I could fashion some skates for the creature out of whatever you have. I'm very handy. I invented the rubber chicken, you know."

The Professor is very handy, indeed. In no time at all he has made a pair of skates for the rabbit-hippo, who is a little nervous as the Professor straps them on his big rabbit-hippo feet.

"What if I'm no good?" asks the rabbit-hippo.

But no one hears him because Dotty Polka puts on some roller disco music.

"Feel the rhythm!" Dotty Polka tells the rabbit-hippo.

Dotty Polka always likes a good student and the rabbit-hippo proves to be a very good student. Oh, there's some booming when the rabbit-hippo falls down, and he crashes through a wall or two learning how to stop on his roller skates. But before long he is roller disco-ing quietly around the rink as if he has been roller disco-ing all his life.

"Look at him boogie," says Erasmus Twiddle.

Boogie, indeed. The creature is so good that Dotty Polka and Professor Piffle catch roller disco fever; they get up and roller disco with the rabbit-hippo.

"Now might be a good time to finish my lunch," says Erasmus, opening his lunchbox and taking out his sandwich. "Maybe somewhere there are people who'll be afraid of a roller disco-ing rabbit-hippo. Maybe there are people who'll be afraid of rabbit-hippos no matter if they hop or roller disco or even if they don't move at all. Some people are afraid of bugs just because they're afraid of bugs, so other people might be afraid of rabbit-hippos for the same reason. I don't mean that people will be afraid of rabbit-hippos because they're afraid of bugs, only that they might be afraid of rabbit-hippos just because they're afraid of rabbit-hippos."

This is very true. And we all know that it is natural for a rabbit-hippo to hop, and that it isn't so natural for a rabbit-hippo to roller disco, even if he is very good at roller disco.

Perhaps one happy day the rabbit-hippo will be able to hop without scaring anyone, and perhaps only then will rabbit-hippos everywhere truly be accepted and loved by the people of Grmkville. But until that day, this particular rabbit-hippo can roller disco, which he really likes to do, and have fun with his new friends.

"That's right," says Erasmus Twiddle. "And while it is very nice to have one friend, it is doubly nice to have two and triply nice to have three. Which the rabbit-hippo now has—three friends: Professor Piffle, Dotty Polka, and me. And it's just the beginning. Many more people will want to be friends with such a big, well-meaning creature who is so good at roller disco. I feel quite certain that the lonely rabbit-hippo will never be lonely again."

a most mysterious mystery
continued

When we last left this most mysterious mystery, Erasmus Twiddle had Travis Plunkett's pants on his head and strange footsteps were hurrying toward him. Well, the footsteps are getting closer and closer, and no matter how hard he tries, Erasmus cannot get Travis Plunkett's pants *off* his head. Believe me, Erasmus is trying very hard to wrestle free of Travis Plunkett's pants, but these are some stubborn pants.

Weevil Kneevil buzzes in our hero's ear, trapped in the pants and finding it a little hard to breathe and—

Uh oh. The footsteps have stopped right beside Erasmus. Travis Plunkett is strangely quiet, which can only mean bad things.

"N'er-do-wells and fare thee wells!" booms a familiar, booming voice. "Alas and woe! Who is it that wears pants so?"

Why, it is only Erasmus's good friend, Bagby Butterbottom. With a flourish, Bagby pulls Travis Plunkett's pants off our hero's head, and Weevil Kneevil flies free as only a daredevil weevil can.

"Excellent Twiddle!" booms Bagby. "What be this, a new fashion craze?" And with that, Bagby Butterbottom puts Travis Plunkett's pants over his own head, wearing them just as Erasmus did, with his left arm in the right pants leg and his right arm in the left pants leg and his face completely covered by the seat of the pants so that he cannot see.

"Allow me to introduce thee to Frances Farkleberry!" booms Bagby from inside the pants.

He bows to Travis Plunkett. But remember, he cannot see. He means to bow to the sad-looking girl he brought with him, who is none other than Frances Farkleberry.

"Twiddle," booms Bagby Butterbottom, "I have broughteth this maiden to see thee and thou because—oh woe be us all!—she has a complainteth of a not-detective variety! Forsooth! Speak, maiden, and I will grieve!" Bagby tries to . . . uh, well, I think he's trying to grieve. I cannot be sure because he's stuck in Travis Plunkett's pants and it's hard to tell what he's doing.

Frances Farkleberry sniffles. "My fleb is gone," she tells Erasmus Twiddle. "I woke up this morning and it was not where it's supposed to be. I can't find it anywhere."

"Hmm," says Erasmus, who wonders where it is that a fleb is supposed to be.

"Have you ever heardeth such a tale of woe!" booms Bagby, who is still trying to do whatever it is he's trying to do.

"I have heard a much worse tale of woe," says Travis Plunkett. "My furgle has disappeared. And I was here first."

"I will now perform a too-dangerous stunt with my weevil-cycle and a cottonball twice my size or my name isn't Weevil Kneevil!" squeaks Weevil Kneevil.

But Weevil Kneevil is not getting as much attention as he likes. Actually, he and his daring cottonball stunt are not getting any attention. Travis Plunkett takes his pants off Bagby's head.

58

Bagby thanks him. Frances Farkleberry sniffles. And Erasmus wonders how he can ask what a fleb is without seeming not to know.

"I have a friend," Erasmus at last says to Frances Farkleberry, "and he never understands what a fleb is no matter how many times I explain it to him. How would you describe a fleb to somebody?"

"Who doesn't know what a fleb is?" asks Frances Farkleberry in disbelief. "It's about yea big . . . " She makes a bunch of strange hand gestures, ". . . and it's got a thingie here and another thingie there . . ." She makes another bunch of strange hand gestures, ". . . and *that's* what a fleb is."

This is really no help at all. But before Erasmus can say anything, Dexter Dumfey runs up and shoves a sack at Bagby Butterbottom.

"Quick, tell me what's in this sack," urges Dexter Dumfey.

"Good sir!" booms Bagby. "There is nothing in your sack!"

"That's what I was afraid of," says a mopey Dexter Dumfey. "That means my grumber has been stolen."

And before Erasmus can ask one of the many not-detective questions that I am sure are on the tip of his tongue, Nubs Carmichael appears clutching an empty picture frame.

"My hojie! Where is my hojie?" cries Nubs Carmichael. "Gone, gone, my hojie!"

And here comes Georgiana Puckerbush saying that her cherished ploff and yonk are missing. And Fred Zuplansky yells into our hero's ear something about his oogoo not being where he left it the night before.

"I am nothing without my fleb," whimpers Frances Farkleberry.

"I am zilcho without my grumber," mumbles Dexter Dumfey.

"I am a lost man without my hojie," moans Nubs Carmichael.

"My ploff and yonk are the most important things in the world to me," confesses Georgiana Puckerbush.

"And I don't see how I can go on living without my oogoo," whines Fred Zuplansky.

Then Travis Plunkett, Frances Farkleberry, Dexter Dumfey, Nubs Carmichael, Georgiana Puckerbush, and Fred Zuplansky start arguing about who got to Erasmus first and whose stolen item should be recovered first, each claiming that their stolen item is much more important than the others.

"Ta-da!" squeaks Weevil Kneevil, who has completed his too-dangerous cottonball stunt to no applause whatsoever.

"Begads! Woebegone quoth I!" booms Bagby. Now that he is free of Travis Plunkett's pants, Bagby puts a hand to his heart, then his head, then his knee. He is grieving, you see, for all the woe in the world.

"I will recover all of your things at the same time," Erasmus Twiddle tells Travis Plunkett, Frances Farkleberry, Dexter Dumfey, Nubs Carmichael, Georgiana Puckerbush, and Fred Zuplansky. "The same thief who took Travis's furgle took Fred's oogoo—not to mention the missing fleb, grumber, hojie, ploff, and yonk. Luckily, I know who the thief is."

"You do?" ask Frances Farkleberry, Dexter Dumfey, Nubs Carmichael, Georgiana Puckerbush, and Fred Zuplansky. "Who?"

"Whoever wrote this poem," answers Erasmus Twiddle, holding up the mysterious poem that was left on his doorstep.

This is not the answer Frances Farkleberry, Dexter Dumfey,

Nubs Carmichael, Georgiana Puckerbush and Fred Zuplansky were expecting. They have never heard of Whoever Wrote This Poem.

"I would like to examine what there is to examine, if I may," says our hero.

And so Erasmus examines Nubs Carmichael's picture frame. Nothing unusual there. It is just an empty picture frame.

"It would be a lot easier looking for clues if I knew what a furgle, fleb, grumber, hojie, ploff, yonk, oogoo, and eebee are," whispers Erasmus Twiddle. "But I must look for clues because that's what not-detectives do. They do not sit around burping and eating pretzels and waiting for clues to come to them. Well, the mysterious poem did come to me, but . . . hey, look at that interesting thing over there."

There is no interesting thing over there. Erasmus just got tired of trying to explain himself. He examines Dexter Dumfey's sack. It looks like any ordinary sack except—

"I found something," announces our hero.

Yes, there is a small hole in the bottom of the sack.

"How'd that get there?" asks Dexter Dumfey.

"A grumber could easily fit through this hole," determines Erasmus Twiddle, who has no idea if a grumber could fit through the hole. But Dexter Dumfey does not say that a grumber cannot fit through the hole, so our hero must be right. "The thief took your grumber out through this hole when you weren't looking, Dexter," says Erasmus Twiddle. "Now I would like all of you to copy a sentence onto a piece of paper. It is from the mysterious poem that I found on my doorstep. Here is the sentence: 'Erasmus Twiddle thinks he's clever, villains and thieves outsmart him never.'"

61

Everyone copies the sentence onto a piece of paper. Weevil Kneevil leaves little weevil prints all over a piece of paper. Erasmus compares their handwriting to the handwriting in the poem. No one's handwriting matches the handwriting in the poem.

"Which means that no one here wrote this poem and so no one here is the thief," concludes our famous and talented not-detective.

So there are eight fewer suspects in Grmkville than there were a minute ago. That is not saying much, I guess. It is only saying that anyone in Grmkville could be the thief—anyone except Travis Plunkett, Frances Farkleberry, Dexter Dumfey, Nubs Carmichael, Georgiana Puckerbush, Fred Zuplanksy, Bagby Butterbottom, and Weevil Kneevil.

"Yes, but the thief has not yet stolen an eebee and in his poem he said he would steal an eebee," says Erasmus Twiddle. "Who in Grmkville owns an eebee and can I get to him or her before the thief does?"

That is an excellent question. But I am afraid you will have to read "The Case of the Exploding Donkey" before you learn the answer. Remember: It is not nice to put your finger in someone else's cream pie. Oops. Sorry. That's from another book. I meant to say that it is not nice to skip ahead to find out what happens next in this most mysterious mystery. You're welcome.

the
case of the
Exploding Donkey

1

Everybody knows that donkeys do not simply explode. Somebody has to make them explode. And everybody knows that it is not nice to explode a donkey. Donkeys do not hurt anybody. Most of the time they just stand around and eat grass and flick their ears to shoo away flies. Sometimes they are stubborn and do not want to work, but that is not a reason to make one explode. How would you like it if someone exploded your dog or cat or goldfish? You would not like it. You would not like it one bit.

Erasmus Twiddle knows what everybody knows—that donkeys do not simply explode. So he is not surprised when the phone rings and he hears Mrs. Carbuncle on the other end of the line. He has been expecting her call.

63

"Erasmus, this is Mrs. Carbuncle," says Mrs. Carbuncle. "Please come over as quick as you can. It's my pet donkey, Reginald."

Mrs. Carbuncle lives down the street from our famous and talented not-detective. Mrs. Carbuncle is not pretty. In fact, she is quite ugly. She is so ugly that she scares Erasmus, even though he pretends not to be scared. Mrs. Carbuncle often gives him tea and cookies so he tries hard not to be afraid of her. She is ugly but not mean. Erasmus likes Mrs. Carbuncle when he is not afraid of her. He knows it isn't nice to say that someone is ugly, but there is nothing he can do. Well, he can say nothing at all,

BUUURF

but he certainly cannot say that Mrs. Carbuncle isn't ugly because she is.

Perhaps you think it strange that Mrs. Carbuncle has a pet donkey. Why not a dog or a cat or a goldfish like everybody else? Well, that is a question only Mrs. Carbuncle can answer. But certain it is that Mrs. Carbuncle loves her donkey as much as anyone has ever loved a dog or a cat or a goldfish.

"Besides," says Erasmus Twiddle, "I have read about people in distant lands who keep crocodiles and ostriches as pets. Why not a donkey? Mrs. Carbuncle is the only person in Grmkville with a pet donkey, but that does not necessarily mean that to keep a pet donkey is strange. Maybe it's strange that the rest of us in Grmkville do not have pet donkeys."

Yes, this is what Erasmus says, but he too used to think it strange that Mrs. Carbuncle had a pet donkey. Even now, he would like to ask Mrs. Carbuncle if she thinks it odd that no one else in Grmkville has such a pet. But he does not ask. He sits in a big armchair in Mrs. Carbuncle's living room and eats a peanut butter cookie. The chair is much too big for him and makes him feel very, very small.

"I don't know," says Mrs. Carbuncle. "He simply exploded."

"Everybody knows that donkeys do not simply explode, Mrs. Carbuncle," says Erasmus Twiddle.

"You make so much sense, Erasmus," says Mrs. Carbuncle. "That is why I called you. Would you like another cookie?"

"Yes, thank you."

Erasmus bites into his fifth peanut butter cookie. He is supposed to know about exploding donkeys. He is supposed to know about mysterious things and an exploding donkey is certainly a mysterious thing. But Erasmus Twiddle has never before heard about exploding donkeys. He does not admit this to Mrs. Carbuncle because it would be unprofessional. He listens with great attention as Mrs. Carbuncle tells him what happened.

"We had a quiet day at home," says Mrs. Carbuncle. "Reginald spent the morning swishing his tail in the backyard. I made lunch and we ate together out at the picnic table. After lunch, I asked him to come inside and help me with my crochet. I am making a plant holder and he held the yarn between his hooves. Let's see—oh yes—then I allowed him to watch TV while I prepared dinner and we ate at the dinner table as we usually do. He helped me wash the dishes because that's the kind of donkey he was—always so kind and thoughtful—and then I went to bed." Mrs. Carbuncle starts to cry. "He liked to stay up later than I do and I suppose he wandered out to the backyard for a midnight snack. I heard this very awful, very loud noise which caused me to jump from my bed in fright. I called Reginald's name but received no answer. I noticed that the back door was open, so I went out to the backyard and that's where I found him, a little of him here, a little of him there. It was not a pretty sight. I am very sad."

Erasmus Twiddle is sad too. He does not like donkeys to explode when they have done nothing wrong. He does not like donkeys to explode at all.

"You must find out what happened," Mrs. Carbuncle says, sniffling and crying into her plate of cookies. "You must tell me who or what made my poor Reginald explode."

"Yes, I will start right away," declares Erasmus Twiddle, taking a last tear-soggy cookie and putting it in his pocket. "First, I would like to see the exact spot where Reginald sat when he helped you with your crochet."

"He sat in that chair there," points Mrs. Carbuncle.

Erasmus examines the cushions of the chair. He finds a few donkey hairs but nothing suspicious. He places the hairs in a plastic jar and puts the jar in his pocket with the cookie. "I will study these hairs later," he says. "Now I would like to see where Reginald sat when he watched TV."

"Well, he sat right there on the couch," says Mrs. Carbuncle.

"And did he cross his legs like this?" asks Erasmus Twiddle.

"No. No, I don't think so."

"Aha!" says Erasmus Twiddle, as if this is important. "And tell me, what did Reginald eat for lunch and dinner? Was it something unusual?"

"Not at all. He ate three cupfuls of grass with a little sugar sprinkled on top. The same as always."

"And one last question, Mrs. Carbuncle," says a determined Erasmus Twiddle. "Could you please show me exactly how Reginald walked around the house? Please retrace his steps from the chair where he helped you with your crochet to the couch where he watched TV and then to the dinner table where the two of you ate dinner. It could be very helpful."

Mrs. Carbuncle gets on her hands and knees and pretends that she is Reginald, the donkey. She crawls on all fours to the chair and then to the couch. She brays at the TV because that is what Reginald did and then she crawls on all fours to the dinner table where she sits in Reginald's usual seat.

"Very interesting, thank you," says Erasmus. "Now I would like to see the backyard, if I may."

"By all means," says Mrs. Carbuncle. "But I would rather not go there myself so soon after the tragic discovery of my beloved Reginald. You know where the backyard is."

"Yes. It is in the back," says Erasmus Twiddle.

"Quite right, quite right," says Mrs. Carbuncle, who, for some reason, is still on all fours in the kitchen, pretending to be Reginald and trying to swish her tail.

2

The first thing Erasmus notices in the backyard is the flower bed. Some of the flowers are blooming and pretty, but most of them have been trampled and crushed. A lesser not-detective might consider the trampled flower bed a clue, assuming that an intruder had not seen the flower bed in the dark and had stepped in it. Whoever's shoes match the footprints in the dirt, why, they had something to do with poor Reginald exploding! Yes, a lesser not-detective might think this, but not Erasmus Twiddle.

"That's right," says Erasmus, "because I have often seen Reginald walk all over the flower bed. Mrs. Carbuncle spends a lot of time caring for her flowers. She loves flowers but she loved Reginald even more, so whenever she caught him tramping on her flower bed, she did not punish him. She only laughed and said, 'Reginald, you bad donkey!'"

It is true. If you look closely at the footprints in the flower bed, you will see that they are not footprints at all. They are hoofprints!

Surely an exploding donkey would make a terrible mess, but there is no sign of Reginald anywhere in the backyard. Someone must have cleaned him up because everything looks perfectly ordinary: the bushes, the garden hose, the picnic table, the fence. Nothing here that should not be here, and nothing missing that should not be missing. But—aha! What's this? A patch of nibbled grass where Reginald must have snacked. And this is very odd . . . a scrap of blue rubber resting in the nibbled grass. Erasmus examines the scrap of rubber with his special not-detective Magnifier Thingie (that is its official name).

"It is part of a blue balloon!" determines our hero. He places the scrap of balloon in his pocket with the cookie and the jar containing the donkey hairs.

"Did Reginald have any balloons that I should be aware of?" asks Erasmus Twiddle, who now stands with Mrs. Carbuncle on Mrs. Carbuncle's front porch.

"Why, no."

"Would you say Reginald was particularly fond of balloons?" presses Erasmus Twiddle.

"I don't think so," answers Mrs. Carbuncle. "Why do you ask?"

"No reason. No reason at all," says Erasmus Twiddle. A famous and talented not-detective must never give anything away. He must keep his methods a secret, even to those he tries to help. "One last thing, Mrs. Carbuncle. I am sorry to ask this question, but did you clean up the backyard yourself?"

"No," answers Mrs. Carbuncle, "I hired the Frangipani brothers to do it."

It would have been better for Erasmus's investigation if Reginald had been left as Mrs. Carbuncle found him. It is always better for a not-detective if a crime scene is left alone.

"But maybe it's better that the Frangipani brothers cleaned up," says Erasmus Twiddle. "I don't really want to see an exploded donkey. It would be gross. One thing is certain, though: At some point I will have to visit the Frangipani brothers, who live in a tree at the Grmkville dump."

3

Mrs. Carbuncle does not own a car or a bicycle and Grmkville residents have often been treated to the sight of Mrs. Carbuncle riding her donkey to Snoots Waterford's grocery store where she purchases milk and cheese. Sometimes, on the way to the store, Reginald would get tired of carrying Mrs. Carbuncle on his back and refuse to walk anymore. There Mrs. Carbuncle would be, sitting on her donkey at the side of the road while cars honked their horns and passed her by. The people in the cars often waved to Mrs. Carbuncle and she always waved back. She never grew angry at Reginald. She would sit at the side of the road for hours and wait until Reginald was ready to carry her the rest of the way to the store.

"I would certainly carry you on my back if I were able, Reginald," Mrs. Carbuncle would say. "But I am not strong enough.

I am an old lady and I get tired easily. It is not even easy for me to walk to the store. Because of this, and because you are strong enough to carry me—well, that is why I am sitting on you now."

Back at home, Erasmus finds his mother sculpting a potato in the kitchen. He has never before seen his mother sculpt a potato.

"What are you doing, mom?" asks Erasmus Twiddle.

"I'm sculpting a potato in the shape of George Washington's head. What does it look like I'm doing? This potato and I are not friends. I'm having a difficult time. It is a terribly disobliging potato. Why don't you go in your room and play?"

A famous and talented not-detective usually plays at not-detective things. In his room, Erasmus takes the peanut butter cookie and the jar containing the donkey hairs from his pocket. He examines the donkey hairs. They are perfectly good donkey hairs that just so happen to be without a donkey. It is a sound conclusion and Erasmus Twiddle rewards himself with a bite of peanut butter cookie. It is not as crunchy as the cookies he ate at Mrs. Carbuncle's house because Mrs. Carbuncle cried all over it and it has been sitting in his pocket. But it is still a very tasty cookie.

"It might be a good idea to make a list of anyone in Grmkville who did not like Reginald," says Erasmus Twiddle.

Yes, a good idea, indeed. It is exactly what he does.

Erasmus Twiddle's List of People
Who Did Not Like Reginald, the Donkey

1. Paramus Plotz

Paramus Plotz lives next door to Mrs. Carbuncle. He has not liked Reginald ever since the day Reginald took a bite of his soccer ball and flattened it and he, Paramus Plotz, could not play with it anymore. Paramus wanted to get a new soccer ball but his mother would not let him. She said she would not get him a new ball because she had just gotten him one and now look, it was ruined. "It was Mrs. Carbuncle's donkey!" cried Paramus. "You cannot blame everything on Mrs. Carbuncle's nice pet donkey," said Paramus Plotz's mother. "I suppose it was the donkey who left your wet bathing suit on the carpet."

2. Henrietta Humphreys

Plump, wealthy Henrietta Humphreys has never liked Reginald because of his smell. "My nose suffers a most unpleasant odor whenever I have the misfortune to sniff that beast," Henrietta Humphreys has often said. And she has always considered it a disgrace to all of Grmkville that Mrs. Carbuncle rode Reginald to the store. "Why can't she get a car or a bicycle like a normal person?" Henrietta Humphreys has often asked. Whenever Henrietta Humphreys saw Mrs. Carbuncle coming down the street, riding happily on Reginald's back and humming a little song, she would pull a perfume bottle from her purse and spray them with perfume as they passed. This always made Reginald sneeze, since he was allergic to perfume.

3. Sam the Sidewalk Sweeper

Sam the Sidewalk Sweeper has never liked Reginald because Reginald sometimes pooped on the sidewalk and Mrs. Carbuncle did not clean it up. Mrs. Carbuncle did not neglect to clean up after her donkey on purpose. She just did not always know that Reginald had pooped on the sidewalk because she would be in the grocery store buying milk and cheese when he did it. But the fact remains that Reginald's poop would be on the sidewalk and Sam the Sidewalk Sweeper did not like to clean donkey poop—or any kind of poop, for that matter—off the sidewalk. "Everyone poops," Sam has often said, "but they do not poop on the sidewalk. We all know it is not polite to poop in such a place, even though sometimes it might be funny. Sometimes poop is really, really funny. Anyway, cleaning poop is not in my job description. I will sweep up paper and bottle caps and things like that, but not poop. Poop of any kind is to be cleaned up by the pooper or a member of the pooper's party. Not by me." Of course, since Mrs. Carbuncle did not clean Reginald's droppings off the sidewalk and there was no one else to do it, Sam often swept them into the gutter.

4. Abel and Barry and Cindy and Darryl and Evelyn and Farrell and George and Harold and Izzy and Jared and Kevin and Larry and Mo and Nancy and Ollie and Perry and Quinn and Randy and Susan and Terry and Ursula and Valerie and William and Xavier and Yolanda and Zachary. The list would have been too long to give all of these people their own numbers. Besides, they did not like Reginald for the same reasons. They have never thought it right for Mrs. Carbuncle to have a pet donkey. They think she should have a dog, even though Mrs. Carbuncle does not like dogs. They also never liked to watch Reginald snack on his candy bars made of grass and caramel, because he always chewed with his mouth open and they thought it disgusting. A donkey without manners is a donkey without friends.

The End of Erasmus's List of People Who Did Not Like Reginald, the Donkey

"I know what I must do," declares our hero. "I must visit each and every suspect on this list, and surely one of them will turn out to be the dreaded donkey exploder of Grmkville."

Yes, let's hope so. Who wants a dreaded donkey exploder running around? Who knows what animals such a fiend might explode next?

4

The first suspect on **Erasmus Twiddle's List of People Who Did Not Like Reginald, the Donkey** is Paramus Plotz. So off our hero goes to visit Paramus Plotz.

"If this is about that donkey," says Paramus Plotz, "and you think I had anything to do with it . . . well, I spit on your parade. Why does everyone pick on me? I'm glad there is no more of that darn donkey—I never liked him, especially after what he did to my soccer ball—but I had nothing to do with him exploding. I didn't do it."

"What is that smell?" sniffs Henrietta Humphreys, the next suspect on Erasmus's list. "You have been visiting Mrs. Carbuncle, I can tell. I know why you are here and I am insulted, horrified that you think I could be capable of any wrongdoing. Of course

74

I will not miss that malodorous donkey, but that does not make me a criminal. Maybe now Mrs. Carbuncle will buy a car or a bicycle. God forbid she should get another donkey! As for you—I have a lot of money, I could make a big mountain out of my money and sit at the top and look down on you. You will hear from my lawyer. Now off you go!"

"Some days I wished that donkey would drown in his own poop," admits Sam the Sidewalk Sweeper, the next suspect on Erasmus's list. "But that's because I was mad. I never would have actually done anything to hurt the fella. I didn't dislike him as much as you think. He was a kind animal—except for the pooping thing."

"Mrs. Carbuncle's donkey exploded? This is the first we've heard of it," say Abel and Barry and Cindy and Darryl and Evelyn and Farrell and George and Harold and Izzy and Jared and Kevin and Larry and Mo and Nancy and Ollie and Perry and Quinn and Randy and Susan and Terry and Ursula and Valerie and William and Xavier and Yolanda and Zachary.

The life of a famous and talented not-detective is not always fun and exciting. Erasmus Twiddle is tired. He has visited every suspect on his list and he does not seem to have made any progress in his investigation.

"It's true," says Erasmus Twiddle. "Sometimes I look at my list of suspects and think everyone on it is guilty. Other times I look at the list and think everyone on it is innocent. I wonder if I forgot to list a person who did not like Reginald, or if Reginald's exploding has nothing at all to do with people who don't like pet donkeys."

So you see, Erasmus Twiddle is willing to think about the situation from all angles, which is important for a not-detective to do.

"Of course it is," says Erasmus Twiddle, "and I will not be discouraged. I still have two people to visit." And with that, he makes his way to the Grmkville dump, where he knocks on a large Frangipani tree.

"Who is it?" ask two voices.

"It is I, Erasmus Twiddle, the famous and talented not-detective," says Erasmus Twiddle.

"We've been expecting you."

And down the tree slide two skinny men with long mustaches—the Frangipani brothers. The Frangipani brothers always talk at the same time, so it is a lucky thing that they always say the same thing; otherwise, it would be impossible to understand them.

"Yes, we cleaned the donkey from Mrs. Carbuncle's backyard," say the Frangipani brothers. "We used our Stupendous Sucker Machine. It's really a vacuum but we like the name Stupendous Sucker Machine. Don't you like the name? Say it."

"Stupendous Sucker Machine," says Erasmus Twiddle.

"What a delightful ring it has! What delicious melody!" cry the Frangipani brothers.

"Yes," says Erasmus, "but about the donkey."

"What donkey?" say the Frangipani brothers. "Don't you want to ask us about the balloons? We want to talk about the balloons."

"Balloons?"

"Yes, so many balloon bits all over Mrs. Carbuncle's backyard that we could hardly find any donkey to suck up with our Stupendous Sucker Machine."

Hmm. Balloons. Very curious. "I would like to see these balloons, if I may," says Erasmus Twiddle.

The Frangipani brothers look at each other. "Well . . . um . . . er . . . we don't have them anymore. We lost them. There was a big gust of wind. No—a fire. Or a flood. No, a giant balloon-loving bird came down and carried them off. Yes, that's it. We have to go."

The Frangipani brothers scuttle back up their tree—high, high up where Erasmus cannot see them. Erasmus would climb after them if he did not have such important things on his mind. The presence of these balloons puzzles our famous and talented not-detective, so he once again puzzles over his list of suspects.

"I have an idea," Erasmus says at last. "I will tell people that I wish to explode an elephant and that I will use either a firecracker or this patented exploding device shaped like a muffin. I will ask which they think is best and . . . oh, I don't want to tell you anymore because it will spoil the fun and suspense. You will see for yourself what happens."

"You again?" sniffs Henrietta Humphreys. "I smelled you coming a block away. Explode an elephant? Don't be ridiculous. One exploding animal is enough for any town."

"Once he's exploded," says Sam the Sidewalk Sweeper, "it will make no difference to the elephant whether you use a firecracker or a patented exploding device shaped like a muffin.

But why do you want to explode an elephant? I thought you were a nicer boy than that."

"Please don't explode an elephant! We like elephants!" cry Abel and Barry and Cindy and Darryl and Evelyn and Farrell and George and Harold and Izzy and Jared and Kevin and Larry and Mo and Nancy and Ollie and Perry and Quinn and Randy and Susan and Terry and Ursula and Valerie and William and Xavier and Yolanda and Zachary.

"Guess what? I'm going to explode an elephant," Erasmus tells Paramus Plotz. "But I haven't decided whether to use a firecracker or this patented exploding device shaped like a muffin."

Paramus Plotz lets out a nasty snicker. "You can't blow up an elephant with any silly old firecracker and those patented exploding devices never work. If you really want to blow up an elephant, I'll tell you what you do. Take a bunch of balloons and fill them with air and feed them to the elephant. Make sure they don't pop. He should swallow them like pills. The elephant's tummy will get full of balloons, so full that the elephant becomes a kind of elephant-balloon. Then you take a pin and—pop!—you pop the elephant. Elephant exploded."

Erasmus is smiling. "Maybe you are aware that balloons were found with Mrs. Carbuncle's exploded donkey?"

"Uh oh," says Paramus Plotz.

"That's right," says our famous and talented not-detective. "You have given it away. It was you who exploded Mrs. Carbuncle's pet donkey. You used balloons and a pin to accomplish your devilicious crime. You have as good as admitted it. Now if you will come with me, I will hand you over to Mrs. Carbuncle."

"I have only one thing to say to you," hisses Paramus Plotz. "Na na na na na na, na na na na na na." And with that, Paramus runs away.

"Mrs. Carbuncle," says Erasmus Twiddle, "I have discovered the person who exploded your donkey and it is none other than your next-door neighbor, Paramus Plotz. He is hiding somewhere in the bushes at this very minute."

"Oh my, those are prickly bushes," says Mrs. Carbuncle.

"Yes, very prickly," replies Erasmus Twiddle.

"I have always known that Plotz boy was a troublemaker," says Mrs. Carbuncle. "Have a caramel."

"Thank you."

The caramel is very chewy and Erasmus spends a long time chewing. His mother would not like him eating candy so close to dinnertime. But what his mother doesn't know, his mother doesn't know.

"Will you be my donkey?" asks Mrs. Carbuncle.

"Um, no, Mrs. Carbuncle. It is quite impossible for me to be your donkey. It is impossible for me to be anybody's donkey. But I know someone who *should* be your donkey. It would only be fair."

And with that, our hero marches into the prickly bushes to find Paramus Plotz. Paramus is not very happy about being dragged out of the bushes, but there is nothing he can do about it. Erasmus is too strong for him. So our famous and talented not-detective stands the no-good Paramus Plotz before Mrs. Carbuncle.

"From now on, Paramus Plotz, you will be Mrs.

Carbuncle's pet donkey," says Erasmus Twiddle. "Here. You must wear this donkey hat on your head and you must wear these hoof mittens over your hands."

It certainly must be admitted that Paramus Plotz looks a lot like a donkey now that he wears the donkey hat and hoof mittens.

"You're not a very nice boy," Mrs. Carbuncle says to Paramus. "Perhaps you'll be a nicer donkey."

5

After a busy day hunting down the dreaded donkey exploder of Grmkville, Erasmus Twiddle returns home.

"Wash up and get ready for dinner," Mrs. Twiddle says to our hero. "Tonight we're having potato-heads of former presidents and green beans."

Erasmus is not sure that he wants to eat anybody's head, even if it is only a potato. But if he doesn't eat, his mother might suspect something. She is a not-detective of sorts herself, and can often tell when he snacks on Mrs. Carbuncle's cookies and caramels, which spoil his appetite for wholesome meals like presidents' heads. So Erasmus and his mother settle down to eat.

"If I didn't know any better," says Mrs. Twiddle, with a little of George Washington in her mouth, "I'd say that thing swishing outside the window looks just like a donkey's tail."

Erasmus looks to the window. Something *is* swishing outside the window and it *does* look just like a donkey's tail. Erasmus excuses himself from the table and heads outside to see what it is. Well, it's a donkey's tail, all right. It is Reginald the donkey's donkey tail! Reginald stands at the side of Erasmus's house, wearing a sombrero on his head and casually chomping on some grass.

"Reginald!" exclaims Erasmus Twiddle in surprise. "But you're supposed to be exploded!"

"I'm supposed to be wha-ah-achoo?!" sneezes Reginald. It is a very powerful sneeze and shakes loose a thick ball of Reginald's donkey fur, which floats to the ground. "I seem to have caught a bad case of that Peruvian hay fever that's going around," Reginald explains. "I feel like I'm falling apart."

Erasmus picks up the thick ball of donkey fur and studies it. "Tell me, Reginald," says our thoughtful hero, "how come you're not at Mrs. Carbuncle's house?"

"Oh. Well, that boy Paramus Plotz came by to give me some nice treats last night and I think I ate too many of them because my stomach didn't feel too good. I was sneezing and burping and all of a sudden I felt something sting and then— bam!—there was a terrible noise that scared me terribly. I ran off and hid in a basket. While I was hiding, I happened to meet some nice basket weavers. We had some exciting adventures and saw some neat things together. I've just been out and about, enjoying myself."

"I see," says Erasmus.

He leads Reginald back to Mrs. Carbuncle's house, where

Paramus Plotz—in his donkey hat and hoof mittens—is helping Mrs. Carbuncle with her crochet. Mrs. Carbuncle takes one look at Reginald and throws her arms around him.

"My beautiful donkey! My poor exploded donkey!" cries Mrs. Carbuncle. "How in the world did you put him back together, Erasmus?"

"I didn't put him back together," explains our famous and talented not-detective. "I didn't have to. He never exploded."

Mrs. Carbuncle makes a face. How could Reginald not have exploded?

"Paramus *tried* to explode Reginald by feeding him balloons and popping him with a pin," explains Erasmus. "But before he could succeed at his devilicious crime, Reginald burped out the balloons and they popped. The loud noise scared Reginald and he ran off. The loud noise is also the explosion you thought you heard, Mrs. Carbuncle."

"But I found donkey bits all over the backyard," says Mrs. Carbuncle.

"Very easy to explain," says our hero. "Reginald has a cold and thick balls of donkey fur shake loose and fall to the ground whenever he sneezes. When you went into the backyard in the middle of the night and saw bits of donkey everywhere, you naturally thought that Reginald had exploded. But he had only sneezed. This also explains why the Frangipani brothers hardly found any donkey bits in the backyard. An exploded donkey would have left many more donkey bits."

"I'll never let you out of my sight again," sighs Mrs. Carbuncle, hugging Reginald tight.

82

Reginald clears his donkey throat. "Ahem," he says timidly, "you know, I did enjoy my brief taste of freedom. Going where I want whenever I want. Seeing new sights and such. I met a lot of swell people—which is how I got this snazzy sombrero. I never realized how much there was to see in the world until now. I have loved living with you, Mrs. Carbuncle. You're an excellent companion. But I think it's time I was out on my own. I need to see the world and have donkey adventures. I can't be tied down to one place anymore. I'm a wanderer."

Mrs. Carbuncle blinks. Reginald does not want to live with her anymore?

"You know what they say," urges Reginald, the donkey, "if you love your donkey, set him free."

Mrs. Carbuncle has never heard the saying *If you love your donkey, set him free.* "Well, if you think it's best," she says, not at all sure that it is best.

But Reginald's bag is already packed and he waves goodbye with his sombrero as he trots toward the horizon. "Adios!" he calls. "Arrivederci! Au revoir! Bon appétit! Benito suona il piano! Ciao! Ciao!" Reginald the donkey disappears over the horizon and Grmkville is less one donkey.

"Where do you think *you're* going?" Erasmus asks Paramus Plotz, who is tiptoeing away in his donkey hat and hoof mittens.

"I didn't do anything wrong," grumbles Paramus. "I'm going home."

"Of course you did something wrong," says our hero. "You *tried* to explode Mrs. Carbuncle's pet donkey. You even thought you'd done it. Trying to explode a donkey is almost as bad as

83

exploding one. You have to be punished for trying to explode a donkey. So you still have to be Mrs. Carbuncle's pet donkey."

"I suppose a two-legged donkey is better than no donkey," sighs Mrs. Carbuncle, looking off at the horizon.

Yes, a two-legged donkey is better than no donkey provided that the two-legged donkey was never a four-legged donkey. Do not worry if you are confused. It is not important. Here is our hero, on his way home to finish his dinner of potato-heads of former presidents and green beans.

"Mrs. Carbuncle will be sad for a while," concludes Erasmus Twiddle. "Nothing can ever make up for the loss of Reginald's company. But at least now she has Paramus Plotz for a pet donkey, which will make her feel a tiny bit better. Paramus will help her crochet. He will trample her flower bed and eat plates of grass at the dinner table. He will bray at the TV and carry Mrs. Carbuncle to the store to buy milk and cheese. He will do everything that Reginald did, and maybe one day Mrs. Carbuncle will love Paramus Plotz almost as much as she loved Reginald, her poor exploded donkey who did not explode after all, but only went off to see the world and have exciting donkey adventures."

a most mysterious mystery gets even more mysterious

We last left Erasmus Twiddle pondering over this most mysterious mystery and, well, things were pretty mysterious. They were so mysterious that I would like to remind you of what's happening. A thief, out to prove that he is more clever than our famous and talented not-detective, has stolen Travis Plunkett's furgle, Frances Farkleberry's fleb, Dexter Dumfey's grumber, Nubs Carmichael's hojie, Georgiana Puckerbush's ploff and yonk, and Fred Zuplansky's oogoo. And it looks like the thief is going to get away with his crimes. Which, I suppose, would make him more clever than Erasmus, since he sent our hero a poem saying he was going to steal these things and he did it just as he said he would and Erasmus hasn't been able to catch him. Yes, people all over Grmkville are starting to grumble that perhaps the thief really is more clever than our famous and talented not-detective. And I do not blame them.

"Thanks for the vote of confidence," says Erasmus Twiddle. "I still have one chance to catch him, you know. In his poem, the thief vowed to steal an eebee—whatever that is. I have been told that Suzy Loopy is the only person in Grmkville who owns an eebee. So all I have to do is hide near Suzy Loopy and when the thief tries to steal her eebee—pow!—I'll be there to catch him."

It is true that Suzy Loopy is the only person in Grmkville who owns an eebee. The thing is, Suzy Loopy is not in Grmkville. She is off seeing the world's largest oven mitt and won't be back until late in the afternoon. Suzy Loopy carries her eebee with her everywhere she goes, so the eebee is off seeing the world's largest oven mitt too. Erasmus cannot catch an eebee-stealing thief when there is no eebee in Grmkville to steal, can he? I do not think so. He would have to be very, very, very, very clever to do that.

Weevil Kneevil whispers in our hero's ear.

"Okay, yes, I see," says Erasmus Twiddle. "Your attention, please. Weevil Kneevil has planned a too-dangerous stunt for our entertainment," our hero announces to Bagby Butterbottom, Travis Plunkett, Frances Farkleberry, Dexter Dumfey, Nubs Carmichael, Georgiana Puckerbush, and Fred Zuplansky. "He will cycle through eleven apples on his weevil-cycle or his name isn't Weevil Kneevil. He would like me to give you these flyers which state that this too-dangerous stunt will take place right here, right now."

This is perhaps not the best time for a too-dangerous weevil stunt. But Travis Plunkett, Frances Farkleberry, Dexter Dumfey, Nubs Carmichael, Georgiana Puckerbush, and Fred Zuplansky hope that the excitement of the stunt will take their minds off their missing furgle, fleb, grumber, hojie, ploff, yonk, and oogoo. So everyone settles down to watch as Weevil Kneevil revs his weevilcycle.

Zoom!

Weevil Kneevil and his weevilcycle take off, straight for the eleven apples lined up in a nice neat row. Thomp! The daredevil bug zips inside the first apple. Our hero and the others hold their breath and—thomp! thomp! thomp! thomp! thomp! thomp! thomp! thomp! thomp! thomp!—Weevil Kneevil at last bursts out of the eleventh apple and is very pleased with himself.

"Hey," says Dexter Dumfey with a frown. "The holes in the apples look just like the hole in my sack." Dexter Dumfey holds the sack up to the apples. It is true. The hole in the sack and the holes in the apples seem to have been made by the same creature.

"Weevil Kneevil stole my oogoo!" shouts Fred Zuplansky.

"I knew his weevil writing looked just like the handwriting in the mysterious poem!" shouts Nubs Carmichael.

"Lock him up!" shouts Georgiana Puckerbush.

And before Weevil Kneevil can escape, Travis Plunkett clamps him shut in a jar and punches holes in the lid of the jar so that he can breathe.

"I didn't do anything wrong," squeaks Weevil Kneevil. But the poor bug is in a jar and no one can hear him.

This is awful. Could Weevil Kneevil really be the clever thief who put the mysterious poem on Erasmus's doorstep and stole so many important items?

(Hint: Maybe, maybe not. Read "The Case of the Furious Elf" and the first six volumes of the *Encyclopedia Britannica*. Afterwards, if I'm in a good mood, I might tell you. Remember: No skipping ahead. I suppose you don't *have* to read the first six volumes of the *Encyclopedia Britannica*, but it wouldn't hurt you if you did.)

the case of the furious elf

1

Elves are happy little fellows, whistling and singing and doing happy elf things all day long. Some elves do elf things at the North Pole while others do them at the South Pole. Some elves do elf things underground while others do them high up in trees or in other places where you cannot see them. Perhaps you are wondering how I know so much about elves, since they are always in trees or underground or other places where I cannot see them. Well, my uncle is an elf (if you happen to be an elf, hello). I am only trying to say that although elves are very, very short and have silly-sounding voices, in other ways they are just like the rest of us. They get sad and grinchy and are not always happy (they are very, very short and have silly-sounding voices, after all). But elves only let other elves see their bad moods. To the rest of us, they are *supposed* to be happy little fellows.

So you can imagine the surprise when a most furious elf appears in Grmkville. It is a day like any other day, Grmkvillians going about their usual business, and all of a sudden there's this furious elf marching up and down the streets. You can tell he's an elf because he's dressed in a funny green outfit, with a green pointy hat and green pointy shoes.

"Make me . . . humph . . . I know you are but what am I," mumbles the furious elf as he marches around Grmkville, a big frown on his little face. And everywhere he goes, Grmkvillians stop and stare.

"There's a new elf in town," says Noodles McDougal.

"Bah!" says the furious elf and kicks Noodles McDougal in the shin. ("Ow! Ow! Ooh! Ooh!" cries Noodles McDougal.)

"I thought elves were supposed to be happy," says Bill, who was once mistaken for a Frenchman even though he is not at all French.

"Humph!" says the furious elf and throws a rock at Bill. (Luckily, the elf is small and can only throw the rock a small distance. There isn't any danger of it hitting Bill.)

"No elf is gonna get *my* rubber chicken," says Mr. Jax, flopping his beloved rubber bird in the elf's direction. (The furious elf makes a face. He does not want Mr. Jax's rubber chicken.)

The furious elf would be something to stare at even if he were not furious. He is an elf, after all, and it is not every day that an elf comes to Grmkville.

"That's right," says the famous and talented not-detective,

Erasmus Twiddle. "And no one knows where this furious elf came from, why he has come to Grmkville, or why he is so furious. That makes him a not-mystery, which is not the kind of mystery where a person says, 'Egad, my muddy boot has vanished. Please help me find my muddy boot,' but is a mystery all the same. I've never seen anyone so short and furious as this furious elf. Actually, I've never seen anyone so short."

It is true. Erasmus has never seen a real live elf. He has only seen them in books and cartoons. How short is an elf? Let's just say that an elf is shorter than you and will never grow any taller.

"I thinketh I have never seen, a thing as lovely as a bush!" booms a familiar, booming voice.

Bagby Butterbottom—friend, actor, lover of pudding—is crouched in a bush next to Erasmus Twiddle.

"Begads!" booms Bagby. "Methinks perchance I spy a figure of unusual sizeth! Most tiny! And looketh at the funny garb he's wearing—that greeneth stuff with the greeneth pointy shoes and matchingeth green pointy hat! Alas!"

"Yes," says Erasmus Twiddle, "the elf is wearing elf clothes. But why are you in a bush, Bagby?"

"I'm a land-pirate and this bush is my vessel! Ahoy, matey!"

Erasmus looks at his friend crouched in the bush. Then he looks at the furious elf. It is going to be a long day.

"Hark ye, Twiddle!" booms Bagby. "How comes this stray elf to be here? Or as Captain Aaargh might have asked many tides ago: Whence elf, laddie?"

Indeed, it is the question all of Grmkville is asking. Well, not really. No one in Grmkville is going around asking, "Whence elf, laddie?" I only meant to say that—

"Thee and woe!" booms Bagby. "I just thought of something. With such an elf as this I can at last performeth the famous play *The Merry Munchkins of Windsor*."

Erasmus is not at all sure that the furious elf would like to be in *The Merry Munchkins of Windsor*. So he does what every good not-detective does when faced with such situations. He says "hmm" and "ah" a lot and looks thoughtful.

"Hmm, ah," says Erasmus Twiddle. And then: "Uh oh," says Erasmus Twiddle, because the furious elf is marching straight toward him.

"Er, I am not afraideth of an elf in funny green clothes," whispers Bagby Butterbottom. "But uh . . . I thinketh I must be very quiet. I would be most happy-eth, Twiddle, if you did not tell yonder elf that I am in this bush-vessel." And with that, Bagby sits quietly in his bush-vessel.

"*I'm* not afraid of a little old elf," says Erasmus Twiddle. "No, sir. I'm not afraid at all."

Yes, this is what Erasmus says, but he takes a good look at the elf's furious face and cannot help wondering if perhaps he's just a little afraid. After all, the furious elf is marching up to him at a furious pace and, well, perhaps, just maybe, this is a killer elf. Erasmus once read about such things in a book called *101 Need-to-Know Things About Elves*, which, it so happens, was written by my elf uncle.

"It wouldn't look good for a famous and talented not-detective to run away from an elf, no matter how furious the elf is," says Erasmus Twiddle.

The elf marches closer. And closer. And closer.

"Not that I'm thinking of running away."

The elf is very close now. Any second he'll be face-to-face with Erasmus's belly button.

"It's just that I think I hear my mother calling, and—"

The elf is right in front of our hero, looking as furious as ever.

"—and uh . . . well, hello elf," says a brave Erasmus Twiddle. He waves.

The furious elf frowns the most furious frown Erasmus has ever seen. It is also the most furious frown that Bagby, hiding in his bush-vessel, has ever seen.

"Ew," says the bush-vessel.

The furious elf squints furiously at the bush-vessel and reaches into the pocket of his elf clothes. No doubt it is for something terrible. Only a killer elf would reach into his pocket like that. But it is too late to run. It is too late to sail away in Bagby's bush-vessel.

"We're doomed!" cries the bush-vessel.

2

Face-to-face with Erasmus's belly button, the furious, killer elf reaches into the pocket of his elf clothes and pulls out an elf peppermint.

"As a famous and talented not-detective," whispers

Erasmus Twiddle, "I must consider: Would a killer elf have a peppermint? A killer elf has all kinds of weapons—an elf gun, an elf knife. But an elf peppermint is not one of them. What we have here is just a furious elf. Not the greatest thing in the world. But better than a furious, *killer* elf any day."

"Ngot ah ooh anging?" demands the furious elf, who is sucking on his elf peppermint.

"Peradventure and woe!" booms the bush-vessel. "It is elf speak. I speak elf speak. Ngot moo moo loaf. Moo moo boing boing la."

Erasmus does not think there is any such thing as elf speak. He looks at the furious elf, who, for a furious elf, is quite enjoying his elf peppermint. It is not polite to eat elf peppermints in front of others without offering to share. Certainly, if Erasmus were to bring elf peppermints to Mrs. Mumuschnitzel's class, he would have to share with his classmates. But enough of elf peppermints.

"I cannot understand a word you're saying with that peppermint in your mouth," Erasmus tells the furious elf.

The furious elf must not like Erasmus's attitude, because he pops *another* elf peppermint into his mouth. Which, of course, makes the inside of his little elf mouth very crowded.

"Ooh nger ngoping foh ah leprechaun mmbe?" mutters the elf. "Oh nges, ess ngony nn ngelf, ngoosay. Ngon't mingeh ngelf ngevbody. Ngy cuddent ngee gen a leprechaun ngoozits on iz pot uff ngole ateh ngen uff a prengy ranbow? Izzenat ngot oor snging? Humph!"

Since you probably do not understand this, I will tell you

what the elf has just said. He said: "You were hoping for a lep-rechaun maybe? Oh yes, it's only an elf, you say. Don't mind the elf everybody. Why couldn't we get a leprechaun who sits on his pot of gold at the end of a pretty rainbow? Isn't that what you're saying? Humph!"

Perhaps there is such a thing as elf speak, after all.

"I'm the famous and talented not-detective, Erasmus Twiddle," says our hero. "I'm known in places as far away as The Land of Rabbit-Hippos. No doubt you've heard of me."

"Ngah!"

"Oh, well . . . I guess that means no." Erasmus is disap-pointed. He stands as straight and tall as he can and this makes him feel better. "Tell me, elf. Did you lose something you cared for very much? Is that why you're upset?"

"Humph! I'm not upset, Raisin Diddle or whatever your name is! I'm furious!" shouts the furious elf, who has now fin-ished his elf peppermints and can shout properly (you see, it was not elf speak).

"Yes, of course. Was something of yours stolen then?"

"Pffft!"

"Hmm," says Erasmus Twiddle. "This will be harder than I thought."

"An elf peppermint wouldn't be a bad thingeth," says the bush-vessel.

"What's with the talking bush?" demands the furious elf.

"Oh uh, don't mindeth me," says the bush-vessel. "I'm just your average talking bush that also happens to be a vessel for a land-pirate. La de da da dum dum. Quite normal, quite normal."

Perhaps the furious elf thinks a talking bush-vessel is normal. Perhaps not. In any case, he pats his pockets as if he has forgotten something and cries, "Egad, my muddy boot has vanished!" and then marches off to kick a few people in the shins.

By now, all of Grmkville is frightened of the furious elf (all except Erasmus Twiddle, of course). Even people who at first thought he was cute and used to say, "Aw, wook at de widdle furious elf, goochie goochie goo," run and hide from him.

"Run and hide from him?" caws Henrietta Humphreys, a very big lady with a lot of money. "I don't run and hide from anybody! I have people who do that for me! But that tiny man is giving a bad name to elves everywhere! Still, he'd make a nice garden ornament! He could hold a lantern and stand very still by my rose bushes! I'll have the grandest garden in Grmkville!"

"I didn't think such a little guy could cause so much trouble," says Sam the Sidewalk Sweeper. "I was sweeping the sidewalk the other day when he grabbed my broom and broke it over his knee. 'Bah!' he said, which I took to mean I was lucky he didn't poop right in the middle of my sidewalk. I was afraid of the little fella, but I don't think I'd be much impressed with elf poop. I've seen the poop of elephants."

"The furious elf is not a pretty sight!" cry Abel and Barry and Cindy and Darryl and Evelyn and Farrell and George and Harold and Izzy and Jared and Kevin and Larry and Mo and Nancy and Ollie and Perry and Quinn and Randy and Susan and Terry and Ursula and Valerie and William and Xavier and Yolanda and Zachary.

"Did the furious elf come to Grmkville to find his muddy

boot?" asks Erasmus Twiddle. "That is a question. Why didn't he give me an elf peppermint? That is another question. I can think of many questions, which is helpful since I'm a not-detective. For example: How many apples does it take to fill the Empire State Building? Why is a horse called a horse? These questions have nothing to do with the not-mystery of the furious elf, I just wanted to show you that I'm good at asking questions."

"What are you saying, you!" shouts the furious elf as he marches back up to our hero.

"I want to show you something, elf," says Erasmus Twiddle. "Come with me."

"Why should I?"

"Oh, no reason," says Erasmus Twiddle.

The furious elf thinks about this. "Well, that's the best reason of all," he says. "I'll do it."

Erasmus looks at the bush-vessel. "Are you coming, Bagby?"

Perhaps Bagby is thinking that he cannot be afraid of the furious elf forever, not if he wants the elf to act in *The Merry Munchkins of Windsor*. Perhaps he is thinking something completely different. In any case, he says, "Yes, Twiddle, but wherever we're going, let us sail there in my bush-vessel!" He makes sailing noises with his mouth. "Swab the branches, mateys! Ahoy! Full leaf ahead!" he booms. But the bush-vessel stays right where it is. "Hmm, I thinketh I have dropped anchor," says a thoughtful Bagby Butterbottom. "We might as well walk."

He hops out of his bush-vessel and walks along with

Erasmus and the furious elf. But they do not get very far before Erasmus stops and whispers in Bagby's ear.

"Right-o, matey! Aaargh!" booms Bagby.

"Elf, you go with Bagby," says our famous and talented not-detective. "I'll meet you shortly. Ha ha. I mean, I'll meet you soon."

"Why should I go with *him?*" demands the furious elf.

"Oh, no reason," says Erasmus.

The furious elf thinks about this. "Well, that's the best reason of all," he says. "I'll do it."

So Bagby and the elf go one way while Erasmus goes another. We, however, are special and can follow them both at the same time.

What Bagby and the furious elf do while Erasmus does whatever he's doing over there ▶▶

Bagby Butterbottom and the furious elf make their way through town as frightened Grmkvillians peer out at them from behind the locked doors and windows of their houses. Bagby glances at the furious elf, opens his mouth to speak, but pretends to yawn instead. He does not know how to start a conversation with a furious elf.

"Uh, I liketh your clothes, furious elf," Bagby says at last.

"Bah!" says the furious elf, and scowls and snorts for good measure.

"Bah! Yes, that's just what I was going to say," says Bagby Butterbottom. "Bah and double bah to you good sir."

It is curious that Bagby does not speak to the furious elf in his usual, booming voice. But perhaps he uses a small voice because he is talking with a small man.

"My name is Bagby Butterbottom," says Bagby Butterbottom. "I'm an actor and a land-pirate. Alas. Aaargh.

What Erasmus does while Bagby and the furious elf do whatever ◀◀ they're doing over there

"Sometimes a not-detective needs to be alone to think over a not-mystery," says Erasmus Twiddle. "And sometimes the best way to think over a not-mystery is to write down everything I know about it."

Taking out his official not-detective pen and notebook, our hero sits on the curb and draws a chart. This is what the chart looks like:

Perhaps you are wondering why Erasmus wrote the word north in a corner of his chart. Well, he wrote the word north in the corner of his chart because he knows that the furious elf entered Grmkville from the north.

"My pretty chart is not helping me as much as I thought it would,"

What be your nameth, matey?"

"Humph!" says the furious elf.

"That's a most strange name," says Bagby. "But alas, maybe it isn't a strange name where elves come from. Walk the plank."

The furious elf hasn't thrown a rock at Bagby or kicked him in the shin. It isn't that scary to talk to a furious elf, after all.

"I say, Humph," says Bagby, "you seem like the kind of elfeth who has done a bit of acting. It so happens that I'm getting actors together to performeth the famous play *The Merry Munchkins of Windsor.* Aaargh and woe. It's the second most famous play in all the worldeth behind *Hamlet's Pumpernickel Loaf.* You would be a most perfect munchkin. Ahoy. I thought we mighteth try a few lines from the play as we walk along."

Bagby clears his throat, sings do re me, me me me, and then, in his best actor's voice, booms:

"Woe-faced munchkin do not be woe,
This littleness you doth wear is but a cloak.
What? I don't know.

admits our hero. "But I won't let it get me down. I will head north, to the very spot where the furious elf entered town, and see what there is to see."

There is not much to see at the north end of Grmkville. No one lives there. No one shops there.

"I have thought of this not-mystery rightside up, upside down and sideways," says our famous and talented not-detective. "The furious elf's muddy boot might be somewhere in Grmkville. But where? When? Why? How? That is rightside up thinking. Or the furious elf's muddy boot might not be in Grmkville. Why not? Where else would it be? That is upside-down thinking. And if the furious elf's muddy boot is not in Grmkville, maybe the elf is here to buy a new muddy boot. Which is sideways thinking."

Our hero has arrived at the north end of Grmkville, where he sees grass, trees, and bush-vessels that would make a land-pirate very happy. Nothing appears to be out of the

A cloak it is, a cloak it be.
Merriness is a virtue in one as small as—"

"Bah!" says the furious elf.

"Begads," says Bagby, "that is perfect. I see that you well know the play, my short, furious friend. You were born to acteth. Let's try another."

Bagby again clears his throat, sings do re me, me me me. In his best actor's voice, he booms:

"Munchkinello, you used to like Jell-O,
But alas, Jell-O fills your dish no more.
Where hath the Jell-O gone?
You be but a munchkin and I be just a man,
Together, however, we make munchkin man."

"Enough of your stinky play!" shouts the furious elf.

"Brilliant," says Bagby. "Most tiny matey, if you have not considered a career in the performingeth arts, I urge you to do so. I knoweth talent when I see it and you, sir, have enough talent for ten elves. But you might thinketh about changing your name. 'Humph' is not very catchy."

Bagby and the furious elf have arrived at Erasmus Twiddle's house, which is exactly where they are supposed to be even though Erasmus is

ordinary as far as grass, trees, and bush-vessels go. But wait. By the side of the road—several broken branches, and a newly made path leading into the woods.

"Clearly, an elf has passed this way," says Erasmus Twiddle. "The broken branches are at exactly elf height."

Erasmus walks the way of the furious elf—that is, he follows the path into the woods. Before long, he comes across his first clue.

"A muddy boot full of elf peppermints," declares Erasmus Twiddle. "Hmm. Clearly, it is the elf's other muddy boot that has vanished."

Farther up the path, our hero finds his second clue.

"A leprechaun with a mustache," declares Erasmus Twiddle.

Not exactly. Tacked to a tree is a picture of a mustachioed leprechaun with several darts in it (someone does not like mustachioed leprechauns). Erasmus measures the distance from the picture to the ground.

"It is at exactly elf height," he concludes.

not at home. The furious elf scowls at the flowers in the yard while Bagby digs through a trunk of Erasmus's not-detective stuff in the garage: Magnifier Thingies, Binocular Thingies, Tape Recorder Thingies, Fingerprint Thingies, and of course, a not-detective rain poncho.

"Avast ye, elf!" says Bagby at last, and holds up a flat, wrinkled balloon.

The furious elf does not care about any wrinkled balloon. He crushes a pretty dandelion under his little elf shoe.

"I will just bloweth a little air into this balloon and we'll be ready for excellent Twiddle when he comes," says actor, friend, land-pirate, and lover of pudding, Bagby Butterbottom. He blows air into the balloon and now we see that it is not a regular balloon at all. It is a punching balloon. It has sand in the bottom, so that when you punch it, it swings to the ground and right back up again. You cannot knock it down. It stands as short as the furious elf and has been painted to look like a clown.

It is, indeed. And if you look over there you will see two small sleeping bags—one green and one rainbow-colored. But what's that? Our hero squints hard at a tree. Did something move? Is someone hiding?

"A true not-detective can visit an elf camp without the elf ever knowing he was there!" Erasmus Twiddle says loudly to the tree. "But it isn't safe to leave a muddy boot full of elf peppermints in the open where someone can take it!"

Erasmus picks up the muddy boot full of elf peppermints and heads back to his house to meet Bagby and the furious elf. But he stops along the way, checks to make sure no one is watching, and hides the muddy boot in a very plain-looking bush-vessel. He takes a single elf peppermint from the boot ("A clue," he says), and puts a nickel in its place in case anyone thinks he is stealing. Once again, our famous and talented not-detective sets out for home. But it is a long walk and he gets hungry.

"Maybe I should study my clue to

"Clown," says Bagby, "Say hello to the furious elf." In a clown's voice, trying not to move his lips, Bagby says, "Hello, elf."

"Hello, clown," says the furious elf, who squints hard at the balloon and furiously chews his elf peppermints.

"Twiddle should be here any minute," says Bagby, who is beginning to wish he had someone to keep him company besides this furious elf. No matter how good an actor he is, the furious elf is just not much fun to be around. "Yup, he shouldn't be too longeth," Bagby says. "La la la. Avast ye, little one, I think I see him now."

Sure enough, here comes Erasmus Twiddle. Bagby waves to our hero and booms in his usual, booming voice: "Ahoy, Twiddle! Yo ho ho! Ahoy, Twiddle! Ahoy!"

Which leaves us to wonder, now that everyone is back together, what our famous and talented non-detective has planned next.

take my mind off eating," says Erasmus Twiddle. He takes the peppermint from his pocket.

"Hmm. Maybe I should unwrap the clue to better study it," says Erasmus Twiddle.

He unwraps the elf peppermint.

"I can't see the clue as well as I should," says Erasmus Twiddle. "I better hold it close to my face to get a better look."

He holds the unwrapped elf peppermint close to his face to get a better look.

"Oops," says Erasmus Twiddle, because the elf peppermint slips into his mouth.

It is a very delicious clue. Erasmus swallows the last of it as he turns onto his street and hears the booming voice of his good friend, Bagby Butterbottom: "Ahoy, Twiddle! Yo ho ho! Ahoy, Twiddle! Ahoy!"

Which leaves us to wonder, now that everyone is back together, what our famous and talented not-detective has planned next.

103

4

"Well, elf," says Erasmus Twiddle to the furious elf, "you're probably wondering what this clown balloon is doing here."

"Yes!" booms Bagby. "Hark ye and ye will hear the saucy-faced elf wonder: Why clowneth?"

Erasmus looks at his friend. Sometimes it is easier to just ignore Bagby Butterbottom.

"Like I was saying, elf," says our famous and talented not-detective, "this clown is a punching balloon. I want you to be as furious as you can and punch it. Punch it as many times as you like and pretend it's the person that made you furious. Afterwards, you might not be so furious and we can talk—civilized elf to civilized not-detective."

"Your breath is minty fresh," says the furious elf. "What have you been eating?"

"Uh, minty fresh things," says Erasmus Twiddle. "Punch the clown, elf."

The furious elf just stands there.

"This clown is wearing muddy boots," says Erasmus Twiddle. "*Your* muddy boots."

"Muddy boots be the clown sportin'! Aaargh!" booms Bagby.

Still, the furious elf just stands there.

"This clown stole your elf peppermints," says Erasmus Twiddle.

"Clown stealeth thy little person's minties! Alas!" booms Bagby.

"Dumb clown," mutters the furious elf, but he still doesn't punch the balloon.

Erasmus takes a fake mustache from his pocket (a not-detective is always prepared) and attaches it to the clown's face. The clown certainly looks a lot like the leprechaun whose picture Erasmus found at the elf camp. The furious elf appears to be more furious than ever before. I think he would have already punched this clown balloon if Erasmus had not asked him to. Why should a furious elf do what anyone asks?

"Tell me again why I oughta punch this ugly balloon," demands the furious elf.

"Oh, no reason," says Erasmus Twiddle.

"Well, that's the best reason of all," says the furious elf. "I'll do it." And with that, he lets loose a mighty swing and punches the clown in the mustache. The mustache flies off and lands on Bagby's lip. The clown pops and shrivels to the ground.

"Do you feel any better?" Erasmus Twiddle asks the furious elf.

"Bah!" says the furious elf. "I've had enough of your balloonigans, Plasmer Fiddle!"

"Yes," says Erasmus, "that is too bad for both you and Plasmer Fiddle. And it is doubly too bad because I'm sure you've had enough of Fugsy B. Whicket too."

"Yes, I have!" shouts the furious elf. "What's a Fugsy B. Whicket?"

"Fugsy B. Whicket is a who, not a what, elf. He's a doctor, the kind of doctor Grmkvillians visit when they're feeling sad or furious and don't want to feel sad or furious anymore. But, as you said, you've had enough of Fugsy B. Whicket. And it's a lucky thing too, because whatever you do, you shouldn't go to his office at 11 Glockbooger Street. It would be absolutely the worst thing you could do."

"Ha! Then that's exactly where I'll go and you can't stop me, Eraser Middle!" shouts the furious elf. And off he marches, straight to 11 Glockbooger Street, which is what clever Erasmus wanted him to do all along.

Bagby, meanwhile, struts around trying out his new mustache. "Begads!" he booms. "This mustache will be a handy part of my costumery for *The Merry Munchkins of Windsor*. With this mustache and yon elf, ours will be the greatest production in the worldeth."

Which gives Erasmus an idea. "C'mon, Bagby. We have to get the Grmkvillians together for a town meeting."

Erasmus and Bagby hurry off to gather the Grmkvillians for the first town meeting Grmkville has ever had. And it really is a good thing we're special, because we can visit with really is a good thing we're special, because we can visit with the furious elf and Fugsy B. Whicket at the same time that we attend the town meeting, where Erasmus Twiddle sets in motion his plan to rid Grmkville of the furious elf, once and for all.

What the furious elf and Fugsy B. Whicket do while Erasmus and the Grmkvillians have their town meeting over there ▶▶

What Erasmus and the Grmkvillians do while the furious elf visits Fugsy B. Whicket over there ◀◀

The furious elf marches into 11 Glockbooger Street and finds a bushy-haired man wearing a half pair of eyeglasses sitting behind a desk. Say hello to Dr. Fugsy B. Whicket.

"I'm here to be upsetting!" the furious elf shouts at Fugsy B. Whicket.

"You fear green netting?" asks Fugsy, who is so hard of hearing that he cannot make out a word the furious, shouting elf is shouting.

"No!" shouts the furious elf. "I said I'm here to be upsetting!"

"Ah," says Fugsy, even though all he hears is that the furious elf fears green netting. He adjusts his half pair of eyeglasses on the bridge of his nose and squints. It is not easy to see out of a half pair of eyeglasses, which is perhaps a good thing. No doubt he would be scared if he knew he had the furious elf in his office.

You are probably wondering why

"Hear ye, hear ye, hi ho the merry-o," says Mr. Jax, flopping his beloved rubber chicken at the assembled Grmkvillians.

"I don't think that's how a town meeting begins," says Noodles McDougal.

"I should think not," says Bill, who was once mistaken for a Frenchman even though he is not at all French.

"Silence, old mateys!" booms Bagby. "You shall let our famous and talented not-detective speaketh or you shall all walketh the plank! Aaargh!"

"Thank you, Bagby," says Erasmus. "Grmkvillians, we have suffered the furious elf long enough."

The Grmkvillians nod, mumble *Yes, we have. Most definitely.*

"And we can't have a furious elf running around our streets forever," says Erasmus Twiddle.

The Grmkvillians shake their

Fugsy does not get a hearing aid or why he wears a half pair of eyeglasses. Well, Fugsy B. Whicket does not think he needs a hearing aid. He thinks he hears just fine, thank you. And as for the half pair of eyeglasses, well, he says they make him look more distinguished than a whole pair. But the truth is, his half pair of eyeglasses used to be a whole pair until he sat on them and they broke.

"Make me!" demands the furious elf.

"Macaroni?" asks Fugsy B. Whicket.

"I know you are but what am I?" says the furious elf.

"You fell in the sewer and hit your eye?" asks Fugsy B. Whicket.

"Why should I?" the elf wants to know.

"I don't think we're getting anywhere," says Fugsy B. Whicket, who cannot understand a word the furious elf is saying. "Let's get back to your fear of green netting. I'll just lie on the couch here and make myself comfortable."

heads, mumble *No, we can't. Definitely not.*

"But as long as he *is* marching around," says Woober Willoughby, owner of the rubber chicken factory, "maybe you could ask him to wear an **I ♥ Rubber Chickens** T-shirt. The publicity would give my business a much needed boost. I'd pay him, of course, as long as he doesn't mind being paid in rubber chickens."

Erasmus does not think this is a good idea.

"We could catch him and put him in the zoo," offers Noodles McDougal.

Erasmus shakes his head at silly Noodles McDougal. Putting the furious elf in the zoo would only make him more furious. Besides, the zoo is not a proper home for an elf.

"Not a proper home for an elf!" snorts Henrietta Humphreys. "Why, he's not a proper elf! He'd make a much more proper garden ornament! I think I'll buy him and have him trained as such! An elf trainer

Fugsy B. Whicket lies on the couch and makes himself comfortable. "I think you should begin by asking about my childhood," says Fugsy. "It was a most happy time—"

"Bah!" yells the furious elf.

"I see," says Fugsy B. Whicket. "Why don't you ask about my dreams? I've had some very interesting ones lately."

"Humph!" yells the furious elf.

"That's what I was afraid of," says Fugsy B. Whicket. "Now say a word and I'll say the first thing that pops into my head."

The furious elf pops a fistful of elf peppermints into his mouth.

"Sleggem!" he cries.

Fugsy B. Whicket yawns and glances at his watch. "My my, would you look at that. Time's up. Shall we say next Wednesday at two o'clock?"

"Say whatever you like," shouts the furious elf and marches out of Fugsy B. Whicket's office.

He marches back out onto the street, all ready to hiss at cats and growl at dogs and do other furious

can be found for the right price!"

"I don't know if the elf is proper or not," says Sam the Sidewalk Sweeper. "But do you think elf babies are smaller than regular babies or do they just stay small forever while regular babies grow up?"

"We're tired of the bully elf!" cry Abel and Barry and Cindy and Darryl and Evelyn and Farrell and George and Harold and Izzy and Jared and Kevin and Larry and Mo and Nancy and Ollie and Perry and Quinn and Randy and Susan and Terry and Ursula and Valerie and William and Xavier and Yolanda and Zachary.

"Grmkvillians," announces Erasmus Twiddle, "the time has come to put on a play. Our stage will be all of Grmkville and every one of us must play a part. I know you are afraid of the elf, but you must be brave for the performance and pretend that you're not afraid."

"Alas and aaargh, Grmkvillians!" booms Bagby Butterbottom. "Prepare to avast ye swabby selves of costumery!"

So the Grmkvillians avast their

110

things. But he stops dead in his little elf tracks. His mouth opens in shock and surprise, and a half-eaten elf peppermint falls onto the sidewalk (Sam the Sidewalk Sweeper will not be pleased). He blinks and rubs his eyes. All because he sees what no furious elf has seen before or should ever have the misfortune to see.

swabby selves of costumery—including one Grmkvillian who is not a Grmkvillian at all and thinks he is being very sneaky. But Erasmus is sneakier and pretends not to notice the fellow. Then everyone heads out onto the street, where they surprise the furious elf with what no furious elf has seen before or should ever have the misfortune to see.

6

The furious elf stands on the sidewalk outside of Fugsy B. Whicket's office, blinking and drooling elf peppermints. He tries to yell "Bah!" but nothing comes out. He struggles to "Humph!" but his voice won't work. He is much too surprised to "Bah!" and "Humph!" Furious elves are everywhere, marching up and down and all around Grmkville. The furious elves look just like him (only taller). You can tell that they are elves because they are wearing funny green outfits with matching green pointy hats and green pointy shoes.

"Bah!" they shout. "Humph!" they cry.

They are not really elves. They are Grmkvillians dressed to look like elves. The furious elf has come out of Fugsy B. Whicket's office to find himself in the middle of a great big production of *The Merry Munchkins of Windsor.*

"Bah!" says Noodles McDougal in an elf outfit. He marches up and kicks the furious elf in the shin. ("Ow! Ow! Ooh! Ooh!" cries the furious elf.)

"Humph!" says Bill, who is not at all French even though he was once mistaken for a Frenchman. Bill, in an elf outfit, throws a rock at the furious elf. (Luckily, Bill's aim isn't very good and there is no danger of the rock hitting the furious elf.)

Mr. Jax comes marching past in an elf outfit. He holds something green and floppy in his hand. It is his rubber chicken, also in an elf outfit.

"Excuse me," the elf says to Mr. Jax.

But Mr. Jax does not want to talk to the furious elf. He shoves his rubber chicken in the little man's face and gives it a flop. "Talk to the elf chicken," he says.

"B-But—" stammers the elf.

"Talk to the elf chicken, you!" shouts Mr. Jax. And with one last flop of his beloved rubber bird, he marches off to "Bah!" and "Humph" with the rest of the Grmkvillian elves.

If you have ever been around a lot of furious elves, or a lot of people pretending to be furious elves, then you know that seeing so many unhappy folks in one place can make you sad. Which is what happens to the furious elf. He becomes a sad elf. And when a roller disco-ing rabbit-hippo whizzes past in an elf outfit that doesn't quite fit, well, it is the last straw. The elf sits down and starts to cry.

Erasmus Twiddle has been waiting for something like this to happen. He takes a seat next to the elf.

"Hello, George," the elf says to Erasmus Twiddle.

Erasmus says nothing and hands the elf a handkerchief to wipe his eyes.

"Thanks," says the elf. "I'm sorry, George. I don't want to be furious. I really don't. I tell my elf self, 'Elf self, don't be furious and act nasty to everybody,' but then I act furious and nasty anyway. I was camping with a leprechaun but we got into a little argument—being little people we get into little arguments—and then he left."

"That would explain the two sleeping bags at your elf camp," says our famous and talented not-detective.

"Yes, well, the next day my muddy boot vanished. I've

113

been all alone with hardly a muddy boot to my name."

"Elf, your muddy boot did not just vanish," says Erasmus Twiddle. "It was stolen."

And with that, Erasmus jumps up and grabs a nearby Grmkvillian elf who, it must be admitted, is quite a bit shorter than all the other Grmkvillian elves. Erasmus takes off the elf's costumery and there, underneath all the elf bits, is a leprechaun with a mustache.

"It's Flanagan!" says the elf.

"Yes, it is Flanagan," says Erasmus Twiddle, as if he has known Flanagan a long time.

"I didn't do anything," says Flanagan.

"We'll see about that," says Erasmus, and gives the leprechaun a shake. Elf peppermints tinkle out of his leprechaun clothes and onto the sidewalk.

"How'd those get there?" asks Flanagan.

Erasmus gives the leprechaun another shake. A muddy boot falls out of his leprechaun clothes and onto the sidewalk.

"Okay, fine," says Flanagan. "I admit it. I took the muddy boot and all the elf peppermints in it. That elf is always talking about how great his elf peppermints are. But has he ever given me one? Nooo. So I did what I had to do. I took 'em and I ate 'em. And you know what? They don't even taste that good."

Erasmus disagrees. He thinks they taste pretty good.

"I noticed Flanagan hiding behind a tree when I visited your elf camp," our hero tells the elf. "And I saw him again at our town meeting. He's been hanging around waiting to steal your other muddy boot full of elf peppermints, which I took and hid for safekeeping. Here it is." He hands the elf his other muddy boot full of elf peppermints.

"I don't know what to say," says the elf. "I . . . I've been a bad elf. Could you stop these people from bahing and humphing all over the place? It's awful."

Our hero stops the Grmkvillians from bahing and humphing all over the place, which they are only too glad to do when they learn that the furious elf is no longer furious. They are not pleased to find that they have a thieving leprechaun in their midst, however. But Flanagan, the thieving leprechaun, is marched off to jail and the Grmkvillians are soon as pleasant and happy as they have ever been.

"Begads!" booms Bagby Butterbottom. "It's just how *The Merry Munchkins of Windsor* ends, with the once unhappy munchkins merry at last!" Bagby is so merry that he hops into the nearest bush-vessel. "Ahoy! Avast ye! Aaargh!" he booms. And then in elf speak: "Ruffenboo! Mug mugla! Aaargh!"

"Elf peppermints for all my friends!" cries the elf.

The Grmkvillians line up to receive elf peppermints from the apologetic elf. Erasmus Twiddle, being Erasmus Twiddle, stands at the front of the line.

"By the way," says our famous and talented not-detective to the elf, "my name is not Raisin Diddle or Plasmer Fiddle or Eraser Middle or even George. It's Erasmus Twiddle."

"Oh, I know," says the elf. "I've heard of you. I came to Grmkville hoping you could help me, but I was too furious to admit it. My name is Ricky."

"It's good to meet you, Ricky," says Erasmus Twiddle.

"It's *especially* good to meet you, Erasmus Twiddle," says Ricky the elf.

Well, another day, another not-mystery solved. Such is the life of a famous and talented not-detective, where furious elves appear shouting about muddy boots, and donkeys explode without actually exploding, and huge, hopping rabbit-hippos boom boom boom into town, and rubber chickens curiously disappear. Who knows what might happen tomorrow?

a most mysterious mystery is still pretty darn mysterious

I never would have thought that a most mysterious mystery could still be pretty darn mysterious after all that has happened. But that's exactly how things are—the most mysterious mystery is still pretty darn mysterious. Weevil Kneevil has been captured in a jar-prison by Travis Plunkett, Frances Farkleberry, Dexter Dumfey, Nubs Carmichael, Georgiana Puckerbush, and Fred Zuplansky. They believe that the daredevil weevil stole their furgle, fleb, grumber, hojie, ploff, yonk, and oogoo. These normally peaceful Grmkvillians have not been behaving in a peaceful manner at all.

"No, they haven't," whispers Erasmus Twiddle. "Weevil Kneevil didn't steal anything, even though some of the evidence points to him. Weevil Kneevil is my friend and I just don't think he'd do something like this. Call it a not-detective hunch."

"Perchance to woe!" booms Bagby as softly as he can. "I have always enjoyed Weevil Kneevil's company and do hopeth that someone else is the thief!"

117

Yes, well, Weevil Kneevil needs more than hopeth. Travis and the others have brought the daredevil weevil to police headquarters for questioning. In a cramped, windowless room, Georgiana sets a microphone next to the weevil's jar so everyone can hear his weevil answers loud and clear.

"So, you wanted a furgle, did you?" demands Travis Plunkett.

"You just had to have my ploff and yonk, eh?" quizzes Georgiana Puckerbush.

"No, no!" squeaks Weevil Kneevil.

"What? Squeak into the microphone so we can hear you," says Dexter Dumfey.

"I'm not a thief!" squeaks Weevil Kneevil getting as close to the microphone as he can, considering that he's in a jar.

"What'd he say?"

"I can't hear him, which definitely means he did it."

"He refuses to squeak into the mike."

"Let's pull off his wings," sneers Fred Zuplansky.

"I DIDN'T DO ANYTHING WRONG!" squeaks Weevil Kneevil as loud as he can. "I'M A DAREDEVIL WEEVIL! I DON'T STEAL THINGS! I DO TOO-DANGEROUS STUNTS! WATCH!"

Weevil Kneevil tries a too-dangerous stunt to prove that he is, in fact, a daredevil weevil. But he flies right into the lid of the jar.

"Wouldn't getting away with stealing a furgle, fleb, grumber, hojie, ploff, yonk, and oogoo be the greatest stunt of all?" asks Travis Plunkett.

118

Poor Weevil Kneevil has nothing to say to this. It would be quite a stunt to steal so many important items and get away with it.

"Caught ya," says Georgiana Puckerbush.

Perhaps you are wondering what Erasmus and Bagby have been doing all this time. Well, Erasmus has been studying the mysterious poem that was left on his doorstep. And Bagby has been looking over Erasmus's shoulder, acting as if he too is studying the poem and mumbling "I say!" and such stuff. Would Erasmus Twiddle let Fred Zuplansky and the others rip Weevil Kneevil's wings off?

"Of course not," says our hero. "Ripping Weevil Kneevil's wings off would be worse than stealing a furgle. But there must be something in this mysterious poem that I haven't noticed before. Its very last line says that the poem itself is a clue. I wonder what the thief means by that. I wonder . . ."

Suddenly, Erasmus's face brightens and he tugs Bagby by the sleeve.

"The only way to save Weevil Kneevil is to catch the real thief," our hero explains to his friend. "And I know who the real thief is."

"We've all heardeth this before, fair Twiddle!" booms Bagby. "The thief is Whoever Wrote the Mysterious Poem."

"Yes, but I know who wrote the poem," says Erasmus. "I know the thief's name. C'mon."

So Erasmus Twiddle and Bagby Butterbottom leave poor, frightened Weevil Kneevil at police headquarters, where he is forced to answer tough questions like, "What have you done with my furgle?" and "Where's my oogoo, you dirty weevil?"

Erasmus, you see, has a plan to catch the real thief. The question is: Can he catch the real thief before it's too late for Weevil Kneevil? Well, I hope you like soggy dumplings because you will have to read "The Case of the Soggy Dumpling" before you find out the answer. Remember: No skipping ahead.

The Case of the Soggy Dumpling

1

Letty Faffenhuffal-Hefenfaffer has been saving her soggy dumpling for a rainy day. Perhaps you are wondering why anyone would want to save a plain old dumpling for a rainy day, let alone a soggy one. Perhaps you are wondering how a soggy dumpling stays soggy if it is left out day after day. Well, these are good things to wonder. I can only say that Letty Faffenhuffal-Hefenfaffer thinks there's no better treat in the world than a soggy dumpling and that Letty's soggy dumpling stays soggy and that's all there is to it. The thing about a soggy dumpling is that it has to be the right amount of soggy. It is very easy to make a dumpling that is too soggy or one that is not soggy enough.

"There are regular dumplings, there are kinda wet dumplings, and then there are soggy dumplings," Letty Faffenhuffal-Hefenfaffer likes to say. "And of all the soggy dumplings in the world, there can be only twelve truly soggy dumplings. A truly soggy dumpling is, um . . . soggy. A person has to taste one to understand."

121

Erasmus Twiddle sits with Letty Faffenhuffal-Hefenfaffer in the school cafeteria, where she works as a chef. It is the middle of a school day and our famous and talented not-detective has been called away from recess to help Letty with an important matter.

"My mother made the best soggy dumplings I've ever tasted," Letty Faffenhuffal-Hefenfaffer tells Erasmus Twiddle. "I used to have twelve, but there have been eleven rainy days and I ate eleven of them. Each one has been better than the one before." She holds up her prized soggy dumpling and lets it catch the light. "So this one, being the last, must be the best of all. I often just sit and look at my soggy dumpling. It's so pretty."

"I don't think the soggy dumpling is so pretty," whispers Erasmus Twiddle. "It doesn't look like it'd taste good either."

No, it doesn't. But that's not very strange. What's strange is that Letty Faffenhuffal-Hefenfaffer frowns. She has never before frowned at her soggy dumpling. Actually, she has *still* never frowned at her soggy dumpling because what she holds in her hand is not her soggy dumpling at all. It is just a piece of paper scrunched into a ball and made to look like a soggy dumpling.

"My soggy dumpling has been stolen," says a sad Letty Faffenhuffal-Hefenfaffer. "And everyone knows that you, Erasmus Twiddle, are the best when it comes to recovering stolen soggy dumplings."

"Yes, of course," says our hero, even though he has never before had to recover a stolen soggy dumpling. "But how can you be sure your soggy dumpling was stolen?"

"You might be a famous and talented not-detective, Erasmus," says Letty Faffenhuffal-Hefenfaffer, "but when you get to be my age you'll know that soggy dumplings don't just disappear. Somebody steals them. Besides, who but a thief would have replaced my soggy dumpling with a scrunched-up wad of paper?"

"Yes, I see," says Erasmus. "May I examine that scrunched-up wad of paper?"

Letty hands the scrunched up wad of paper to our hero. He bites it. It is paper, all right. But now it is soggy paper. Erasmus unscrunches the scrunched-up wad of soggy paper.

"This paper has been torn from a larger piece," he says. "And there is something printed on it: E-R-F. I don't know what E-R-F means. I'll have to keep the paper as a clue. Tell me more about this stolen soggy dumpling."

"Well," says Letty Faffenhuffal-Hefenfaffer, "I was working here in the kitchen this morning. There was no one here but me. I had to pick up a few things at Snoots Waterford's grocery store, so I said goodbye to my soggy dumpling and away I went. I was gone for exactly one hour—from eight o'clock until nine o'clock. When I came back I wanted to say hello to my soggy dumpling. I went to take it from its hammerproof case on top of the refrigerator, and that's when I found out it'd been stolen. I paid quite a lot of money for that hammerproof glass, but as you can see, the thief didn't try to break the glass with a hammer. The thief simply opened the latch, which was unlocked, and took my soggy dumpling, then put the scrunched-up wad of paper in its place."

"Hmm," says Erasmus Twiddle. It might have been better if Letty had kept the hammerproof case locked. But hey, it is not our hero's place to tell Letty Faffenhuffal-Hefenfaffer how to take care of her soggy dumpling. "Can you think of anyone who might want to steal your soggy dumpling?" asks our famous and talented not-detective.

"Who wouldn't?" says Letty.

"Yes, I see your point," says Erasmus, although he doesn't see the point at all. "I'd better take a look around."

"How about a fishsicle before you get started?" asks Letty Faffenhuffal-Hefenfaffer.

"Um, no thank you," answers Erasmus. "I'm not hungry."

"I think I have a few eggsicles left."

"No. Thank you. Really," says Erasmus.

"Well, I think *I'll* have an eggsicle," says Letty Faffenhuffal-Hefenfaffer. And she takes an eggsicle from the freezer and starts licking it.

Perhaps you are wondering what an eggsicle is. Or a fishsicle, for that matter. Well, if a fudgsicle is frozen fudge on a stick, then an eggsicle must be frozen egg on a stick and a fishsicle frozen fish on a stick. Which is exactly what they are. Letty loves to make frozen treats such as eggsicles, fishsicles, meatsicles, bananasicles, liversicles, prunesicles, and picklesicles. You name a food, Letty Faffenhuffal-Hefenfaffer has made a sicle out of it. But unlike fudgsicles, you won't find these treats in your grocer's freezer. They are gourmet foods, which means that people who know a lot about food think they are much better than fudgsicles. Erasmus does not think so. He would rather have a fudgsicle or one of Mrs. Carbuncle's peanut butter cookies any day.

"I am now examining the top of the refrigerator," says Erasmus Twiddle, as he examines the top of the refrigerator.

"I am now examining the soggy dumpling's hammerproof case," says Erasmus Twiddle, as he examines the soggy dumpling's hammerproof case.

"I don't think I should keep telling you what I'm examining when I'm examining it," says Erasmus Twiddle. "It's silly."

Very true. So Erasmus examines all of Letty's pots, pans, dishes, glasses, and silverware without saying a word about it. He looks in every cupboard and on every shelf. He even pokes his head in the trash.

"I don't know what I'm looking for," says our hero. "But a not-detective often doesn't know what he's looking for until he finds it. Aha. Soggy dumpling tracks."

Yes, a path of soggy splotch marks leads out the back door of the cafeteria.

"Don't fret, Mrs. Faffenhuffal-Hefenfaffer," says our hero. "There has never been a soggy dumpling that I haven't returned to its rightful owner."

Which, strictly speaking, is true, since Erasmus has never before had to recover a stolen soggy dumpling.

"Feared and loathsome soggy dumpling thief, here I come," says brave Erasmus Twiddle. He follows the soggy dumpling tracks out the door, no doubt heading straight to the feared and loathsome soggy dumpling thief of Grmkville.

2

Recess is in full swing as Erasmus follows the soggy dumpling tracks down a cement path to the playground, where he finds—

Nothing. The soggy dumpling tracks have faded in the hot sun.

"Not good," says Erasmus Twiddle. "Not good at all."

It is true. Things could be going better.

"Whatcha doin', Erasmus?"

Erasmus turns and sees a freckle-faced girl with her own sun shining down on her. The girl is Lolly Gallagher. Not only does Lolly have her own sun, she has her own clouds too. Lolly Gallagher, you see, has her own weather. If she is happy, her sun shines down on her. If she is angry or upset, clouds form above her head and lightning flashes and thunder roars. If she is sad, the clouds pour down rain. Sometimes it is raining on Lolly Gallagher while it is bright and sunny on whoever happens to be standing next to her.

"Earth to Erasmus," says Lolly Gallagher. "I asked whatcha doin'."

"Nothing," says Erasmus. "Just some dangerous not-detective stuff."

"Oops," says Lolly Gallagher, "I seem to have dropped my

pencil accidentally on purpose."

Lolly always does stuff like this. And Erasmus, being a polite not-detective, always picks up whatever Lolly drops accidentally on purpose. He picks up Lolly's pencil and hands it to her.

"Thank you," says Lolly Gallagher, her little sun shining brighter than ever. "I have something for you." She hands our hero a note. It is not really a note. There's only a picture on it, which looks like this:

"Uh, yes, well," says Erasmus Twiddle, and stuffs the note in his pocket.

"See ya," Lolly says, and skips off to her girlfriends, Mel Mel and Frances Farkleberry. Mel Mel points at Erasmus and they all giggle.

"What's so funny?" wonders Erasmus. "What are they giggling about? Who is Lolly Gallagher anyway? Just some stupid girl with her own sun. Big deal."

A grinchy Erasmus looks off at the jungle gym where Bagby Butterbottom and Ricky the elf are playing a game of pin the tail on Paramus Plotz.

"I can't let grinchiness get in the way of not-detective business," says our famous and talented not-detective. "How were the soggy dumpling tracks made? Maybe the thief is clumsy and kept dropping the soggy dumpling. Or maybe the thief is weak and found the soggy dumpling too heavy and had to keep putting it down to rest. Or maybe the soggy dumpling itself is the thief. The soggy dumpling hopped off on its own and . . . no, that wouldn't explain the scrunched-up wad of paper sitting in Letty's hammerproof case pretending to be a soggy dumpling."

Which reminds Erasmus of his important clue. He reaches into his pocket and pulls out the unscrunched scrunched up wad of paper.

"That's strange," says our famous and talented not-detective. "Instead of the letters E-R-F, this paper now has the letters E-R-F-O printed on it."

Strange, indeed. How could the letters have changed? Erasmus reaches into his pocket and pulls out another piece of paper. This one has the letters E-R-F printed on it. Erasmus turns the E-R-F-O paper over. It's the note from Lolly Gallagher.

"This means that Lolly Gallagher is a suspect," declares Erasmus Twiddle. And until recess is over and everyone files back into class, our hero stares at Lolly as only a not-detective can stare at a girl with her own weather.

"It's Thursday and everyone knows what Thursday means," says Mrs. Mumuschnitzel, once everyone is seated in class.

Paramus Plotz raises a hoof mitten. "It means that it's not Monday, Tuesday, Wednesday, Friday, Saturday, or Sunday. Duh."

"Very good, Paramus," says Mrs. Mumuschnitzel. "It also means that one of you gets to come up here and teach while I play student. Erasmus, do you feel like teaching today?"

Erasmus does not feel like teaching today. But this might be a chance to get Lolly Gallagher to admit that she stole the soggy dumpling. So he makes his way to the front of the room. Mrs. Mumuschnitzel hands him a history book and says he should read to the class about the pilgrims who came to America.

"History," reads Erasmus Twiddle, "teaches us about, uh . . . about many SOGGY DUMPLING!"

He looks hard at Lolly Gallagher. She smiles. Her sun twinkles. She is not acting like a thief. But how is a thief supposed to act? Well, not like Lolly Gallagher.

"And so," continues Erasmus, "history says there were these pilgrims and they were . . . were SOGGY and DUMPLING-like."

Again, he looks hard at Lolly Gallagher. Lolly's sun clouds over, but she bites her lip and says nothing. Erasmus is disappointed. Surely, any thief would admit her crime when faced with such a fierce not-detective.

"Go on, Erasmus. This is very educational," says Mrs. Mumuschnitzel.

Erasmus carries the history book up to Lolly Gallagher and puts his face close to hers. "So these SOGGY DUMPLING pilgrims were not happy where they were SOGGY and they sailed to DUMPLING America on a SOGGY DUMPLING! They landed at SOGGY Plymouth

129

DUMPLING and SOGGY DUMPLING SOGGY DUMPLING SOGGY DUMPLING!"

Erasmus sure is tough on Lolly—yelling in her face like this. Lolly's clouds darken and then there's a little crash of thunder and it starts to rain on her head. Embarrassed, Lolly runs out of the room.

"Well, class, what have we learned today?" asks Mrs. Mumuschnitzel.

Bagby Butterbottom stands. In his best actor's voice, he booms: "Fair Mrs. Schnitzel of the Mumu variety, I think I speaketh for everyone when I say begone bygones and alas! I have learnedeth many a thing about a soggy dumpling! Woe! I have learned that you can saileth on a soggy dumpling, which is a goodeth thing for a land-pirate to know! Gimme my peg leg, aaargh!"

Bagby takes a bow and everyone claps. Everyone except Erasmus Twiddle, who thinks that Lolly Gallagher might not be the soggy dumpling thief, after all. There are still many questions that need to be answered. So it is a lucky thing that Lolly Gallagher waits for our hero after school.

"You were very mean to shout at me about soggy dumpling people, Erasmus Twiddle," says Lolly Gallagher. She frowns and the clouds over her head roar with thunder and flash with lightning.

"Oh, but I guess it's okay to giggle and point at me and I guess you don't know anything about Letty Faffenhuffal-Hefenfaffer's soggy dumpling either," says Erasmus Twiddle.

"I know that it's soggy," says Lolly, very firmly.

She is trying to trick him. He must surprise her.

"O-ho, look what I found," says Erasmus, holding up Lolly's note. He shows her the letters E-R-F-O printed on the back of the note. "Except for the 'O' it is exactly the same as the letters on this piece of paper which has the letters E-R-F printed on it. This E-R-F paper was taken from the very spot where Letty Faffenhuffal-Hefenfaffer's soggy dumpling was stolen. What do you say to that?"

"I say big whoop," says Lolly Gallagher. "They're just scraps of paper bags that came from Snoots Waterford's grocery store."

"Exactly!" says Erasmus Twiddle, although he didn't know this.

"You're weird, Erasmus," says Lolly Gallagher and storms off.

Erasmus does not like being called weird. Perhaps some other time he will chase after Lolly and tell her that he isn't weird, he's just a not-detective trying to do his not-detective job, which isn't always easy. But right now he has more important things to do. *Grocery bags from Snoots Waterford's store?* Everyone in Grmkville has grocery bags from Snoots Waterford's store.

"Yes," says Erasmus Twiddle. "Even my mom uses them as trash bags."

She certainly does. Erasmus races home and digs one of these bags out of a kitchen drawer. And there, printed on the grocery bag for anyone to see, is:

Snoots Waterford's Grocery Because You Eat

As you might have noticed, the letters E-R-F are in E-R-F-O and the letters E-R-F-O are in Snoots Waterford's own name. It is perfectly all right if you did not notice that the letters E-R-F-O are in Snoots Waterford's name, because that is what I'm here for—to tell you.

"Is that you, Erasmus?" calls Erasmus Twiddle's mother, Mrs. Twiddle. "Wash up. We've been invited to Letty Faffenhuffal-Hefenfaffer's for dinner."

"Good," says Erasmus Twiddle. "Because I have a few questions for her."

3

Letty Faffenhuffal-Hefenfaffer is the best cook in Grmkville and Grmkvillians have often gathered to hear her talk about her soggy dumpling. Many Grmkvillians have even tried to make their own soggy dumplings. Noodles McDougal is one such Grmkvillian. He cooked up a dozen dumplings and sprinkled water over them.

"You call those soggy dumplings?" Letty Faffenhuffal-Hefenfaffer said. "Uh-uh. Not soggy enough."

Mrs. Ploppityplop is another such Grmkvillian. She cooked up a dozen dumplings and sprayed them with a hose.

"You call those soggy dumplings?" Letty Faffenhuffal-Hefenfaffer said. "I call them soggy-soggy."

Letty Faffenhuffal-Hefenfaffer is the only person in Grmkville who has tasted a truly soggy dumpling and many Grmkvillians are jealous of her. Many Grmkvillians would like to get their hands on Letty Faffenhuffal-Hefenfaffer's soggy dumpling and be the only *other* person in Grmkville who has tasted a truly soggy dumpling.

"Yes, indeedy," says Erasmus Twiddle. "Lolly Gallagher is one suspect. But Noodles McDougal and Mrs. Ploppityplop are suspects too. There are a lot of suspects. The soggy dumpling is no rubber chicken."

"No rubber chicken!" guffaws Henrietta Humphreys, the wealthiest and waddlingest woman in Grmkville. "Thank heavens! Could you imagine a soggy rubber chicken dumpling? Hideous! If it weren't for me, Letty Faffenhuffal-Hefenfaffer wouldn't even know a soggy dumpling from a rubber chicken! I'm the one who told her mother about soggy dumplings in the first place! I don't know why you're always saying Letty Faffenhuffal-Hefenfaffer is the only person who's eaten one! I've eaten one! Don't you know who I think I am?"

"I'm sure I'd like the taste of a soggy dumpling," says Sam the Sidewalk Sweeper. "I like soggy cereal and soggy bread. But not as much as prunesicles. There's nothing better than a good prunesicle on a hot day."

"Soggy dumplings, yum!" cry Abel and Barry and Cindy and Darryl and Evelyn and Farrell and George and Harold and Izzy and Jared and Kevin and Larry and Mo and Nancy and Ollie and Perry and Quinn and Randy and Susan and

Terry and Ursula and Valerie and William and Xavier and Yolanda and Zachary.

Erasmus and his mother sit at Letty Faffenhuffal-Hefenfaffer's dinner table. Letty is in the kitchen getting the food, but Letty's husband is at the table. His name is Hughley Hefenfaffer.

"It can't be," Hughley Hefenfaffer says to Mrs. Twiddle. "I think you're right. But then again, who's to say? Perhaps. Perhaps not. And yet. Quite possibly. No, it can't be. I mean, yes."

"Voilà!" says Letty Faffenhuffal-Hefenfaffer, coming out of the kitchen and placing a dish of green, icky stuff on the table. "I call it spinach-a-go-go," Letty announces, looking pleased.

Erasmus wishes the spinach would go-go all the way off the table and out the door, never to be seen again.

"And guess what we're having for dessert," says Letty Faffenhuffal-Hefenfaffer. "Hamsicles dipped in chocolate!"

"Mmm, my favorite," says Hughley Hefenfaffer.

"Uh, may I talk to you in the kitchen?" Erasmus Twiddle asks Letty Faffenhuffal-Hefenfaffer. And off the two of them go to the kitchen, where Letty moans and looks sad.

"All my smiling and cheerfulness is an act," admits Letty Faffenhuffal-Hefenfaffer. "I'm very upset. Whenever something bad happens like this soggy dumpling business, I keep active in the kitchen and try not to think about it. This afternoon I made two dozen hamsicles."

"No matter how many hamsicles you make, it will not bring back your soggy dumpling," says Erasmus Twiddle. Which does not make Letty Faffenhuffal-Hefenfaffer any happier. "I'm sure you remember that scrunched-up wad of paper that was in your hammerproof case pretending to be a soggy dumpling," says our hero. "But did you know that it came from Snoots Waterford's grocery store? It was torn from one of Snoots's grocery bags."

"I . . . no," says Letty Faffenhuffal-Hefenfaffer.

"You brought groceries home from the store in those bags," says Erasmus. "Isn't it possible, Letty Faffenhuffal-Hefenfaffer, that you stole your own soggy dumpling?"

"Never!" cries Letty Faffenhuffal-Hefenfaffer, and puts a cold turkey leg against her eye to keep from fainting.

"Yes, of course," says Erasmus. "Just checking. Well then, you are usually at the school cafeteria from eight until nine in the morning. So whoever stole your soggy dumpling must've known that you were not at the school cafeteria from eight until nine this morning. Therefore, the thief was at Snoots Waterford's grocery store with you, because only the people at Snoots Waterford's grocery store could have known that you were not at the school from eight until nine in the morning. Who was at the store with you?"

"Let's see," says Letty Faffenhuffal-Hefenfaffer, fanning herself with the turkey leg, "there was Snoots Waterford. And Zug, who packed up my groceries and carried them back to school for me. Oh, and Noodles McDougal and Mrs. Ploppityplop."

"Hmm," says Erasmus Twiddle. "Was Lolly Gallagher there? And tell me, was she giggling?"

135

"I didn't see her," says Letty Faffenhuffal-Hefenfaffer. "Could we discuss this after dinner? My spinach-a-go-go is getting cold."

So Letty Faffenhuffal-Hefenfaffer and our hero go-go back to the dinner table where Hughley Hefenfaffer is telling Mrs. Twiddle: "Well, yes. Most certainly. Then again, I'm not so sure. I mean, absolutely I see your point exactly. But not at all, really."

"I hate to be a dinner pooper," says Erasmus. "But at this very moment the soggy dumpling thief could be escaping from Grmkville. So if you'll excuse me . . ."

"We'll do no such thing," says Mrs. Twiddle.

Which just goes to show you that even a famous and talented not-detective must put off not-detective business to eat his vegetables, even if those vegetables are green and icky-looking and called spinach-a-go-go, and a feared and loathsome soggy dumpling thief is loose on the streets with his soggy spoils.

4

Erasmus wakes early the next morning and drinks lots of water to wash the lingering taste of a spinach-a-go-go and hamsicle dinner out of his mouth.

"And now I'm off to question Snoots Waterford, Zug, Noodles McDougal, and Mrs. Ploppityplop," says Erasmus Twiddle. "Here I am, on my way to Snoots Waterford's grocery store. Dum de dum dum du—"

"Ahoy, Twiddle!" booms a familiar, booming voice.

It's Bagby Butterbottom and he's with Ricky the elf. Bagby wears an odd assortment of capes and belts. And Ricky the elf is not dressed in his usual elf clothes—that funny green outfit with the matching green pointy shoes and green pointy hat. No, Ricky the elf is dressed in something altogether *different*.

"Fair Twiddle!" booms Bagby Butterbottom. "That was a most excellent history lesson you gaveth yesterday on the soggy dumpling! Alas!"

"What're you guys wearing?" asks Erasmus Twiddle.

"Ah yes! No doubteth you are referring to our costumery!" booms Bagby. "We are off to practice the play *All's Well that Ends with a Mutton Chop!* Aaargh! You are welcome to come along, Twiddle! Elf here is playing the mutton chop!"

Erasmus stares at the elf's mutton chop costumery. Mostly, he stares at the bit of mutton chop costumery on the elf's nose. He picks it off the elf's nose.

"This is Letty Faffenhuffal-Hefenfaffer's soggy dumpling!" declares Erasmus Twiddle.

"I thought it was kinda mushy," says Ricky the mutton-chop elf.

"I never figured *you* would've stolen Letty Faffenhuffal-Hefenfaffer's soggy dumpling, elf. You must come with me and be punished."

"But I didn't steal anything," says Ricky the mutton-chop elf.

"Aaargh, Twiddle!" booms Bagby. "The most teensy mutton chop speaks the truth! I was with him when he foundeth the costumery you so lovingly call dumpling! We'll showeth you!"

And so Erasmus Twiddle, Bagby Butterbottom, and Ricky the mutton-chop elf walk to a shady alley.

"Zounds and peg leg!" booms Bagby, which, I think, means that this is where Ricky the mutton-chop elf found the soggy dumpling. Sure enough, if you look closely, you will see three soggy dumpling tracks. The alley is so shady that the tracks have not yet dried.

"Hmm," says Erasmus Twiddle. "These soggy dumpling tracks are going in a very different direction from the ones I found yesterday."

And while our hero thinks about why there might be two sets of soggy dumpling tracks going in different directions, he happens to look up and see the back of Snoots Waterford's grocery store.

"Will you be keepingeth that bit of costumery, Twiddle?" booms Bagby Butterbottom. "By which, heretofore and thus and such, I mean, will you be keepingeth the mutton chop's nose costumery?"

"I'm afraid so," says Erasmus.

"Sad it is, hark ye! But we'll manage! Come, mutton chop, away with us!"

And off Bagby Butterbottom and Ricky the mutton-chop elf go to rehearse *All's Well that Ends with a Mutton Chop*. Erasmus pockets the soggy dumpling and continues on to Snoots Waterford's grocery store.

"Ah, Mr. Twiddle," says the kindly Snoots Waterford, who is out front of the store blowing his nose.

Erasmus stares at Snoots as only a suspicious not-detective can stare at a grocer blowing his nose.

"I see that you are staring at my snotty handkerchief," says Snoots Waterford. "Would you like it?"

"No, thank you," says Erasmus Twiddle. "You're having a sale on green beans, aren't you? SOGGY DUMPLING!"

"Uh, yes, I *am* having a sale," says Snoots Waterford, "but I don't know what a soggy dumpling has to do with it."

Noodles McDougal and Mrs. Ploppityplop happen to pass by.

"Just the people I wanted to see," says Erasmus Twiddle. He looks at the sky. "I wonder if it'll rain SOGGY DUMPLING tomorrow."

Noodles McDougal and Mrs. Ploppityplop look at the sky. "We hope it doesn't rain soggy dumplings," they say.

That leaves Zug. Erasmus marches into Snoots Waterford's grocery store and stares at Zug as only a suspicious not-detective can stare at a boy shelving potato chips.

"Tell me," Erasmus asks Zug, "do you have canned SOGGY DUMPLING?"

Zug stops what he's doing. Erasmus and Zug look at each other for a long minute.

"Aisle three," Zug says at last.

"Thank you," says Erasmus. But our hero does not go to aisle three to find the canned soggy dumplings. Why should he? He has figured out who the soggy dumpling thief is.

"Of course I have," says Erasmus Twiddle. "But sometimes a not-detective's job is not only to *find out* who did what, but to *prove* that who did what actually did what. Before Letty Faffenhuffal-Hefenfaffer has time to make a dozen eggsicles, I will prove that the feared and loathsome soggy dumpling thief of Grmkville is, in fact, the feared and loathsome soggy dumpling thief of Grmkville."

5

"Mrs. Faffenhuffal-Hefenfaffer," says Erasmus Twiddle, "you must go to Snoots Waterford's grocery store and do exactly what you did yesterday morning when your soggy dumpling was stolen. Buy the same groceries and make the same chitchat with Snoots Waterford, Noodles McDougal, and Mrs. Ploppityplop."

"What if Noodles McDougal and Mrs. Ploppityplop aren't there?"

"Don't ask silly questions, Mrs. Faffenhuffal-Hefenfaffer," says Erasmus Twiddle. "And be sure to have Zug carry your groceries back to the cafeteria here just like you did yesterday morning. I will hide in this cupboard."

"Should I say goodbye to my soggy dumpling?" Letty asks.

"Yes, good idea," says Erasmus. He scrunches up a piece of paper and puts it in the hammerproof case.

"Goodbye, soggy dumpling," Letty Faffenhuffal-Hefenfaffer says to the scrunched-up wad of paper in the hammerproof case. She blows the scrunched-up wad of paper a kiss and leaves.

Perhaps you think Erasmus is mean not to tell Letty that he has found her soggy dumpling. Well, he isn't mean. He just has a plan.

140

"I sure do," says Erasmus Twiddle. "And now that Mrs. Faffenhuffal-Hefenfaffer is gone, I will replace the scrunched-up wad of paper with the real soggy dumpling."

And that is exactly what he does. Then he climbs into a cupboard, which is not a comfortable place for a famous and talented not-detective to be.

"It isn't a comfortable place for anybody to be!" squawks Henrietta Humphreys, who is much too large to fit in any cupboard. "Soggy dumpling schmoggy dumpling! I'm sick of hearing about it! Can you buy anything with a soggy dumpling? Can you put a soggy dumpling in the bank and let it earn interest? It is just a glop of wet food! I'd rather have money any day! Silly me! I *have* money!"

"The difference between a popsicle and a poopsicle is the letter 'O,'" says Sam the Sidewalk Sweeper. "But a popsicle probably tastes better than a poopsicle. I've never eaten a poopsicle."

"We wouldn't want to hide in a cupboard! Especially with a poopsicle!" cry Abel and Barry and Cindy and Darryl and Evelyn and Farrell and George and Harold and Izzy and Jared and Kevin and Larry and Mo and Nancy and Ollie and Perry and Quinn and Randy and Susan and Terry and Ursula and Valerie and William and Xavier and Yolanda and Zachary.

"I wish Letty and Zug would hurry up," says Erasmus. "It's no fun being in a cupboard."

I don't imagine it is. Luckily, here are Letty and Zug now. Zug carries the groceries into the cafeteria.

"Thank you, Zug," says Letty Faffenhuffal-Hefenfaffer, and busies herself with the groceries.

Zug frowns. He eyes the soggy dumpling's hammerproof case, surprised to see what he sees there. While Letty's back is turned, Zug rips a bit of paper from a Snoots Waterford grocery bag and scrunches it into the shape of a soggy dumpling. He reaches up above the refrigerator, opens the hammerproof case, snatches the real soggy dumpling, and is putting the scrunched-up wad of paper in its place when—

"Gotcha!" says Erasmus, jumping out of the cupboard. "You, Zug, are the feared and loathsome soggy dumpling thief of Grmkville."

It is true: Zug is the feared and loathsome soggy dumpling thief of Grmkville.

"But why would he want to steal a scrunched-up wad of paper?" asks Letty.

"It is not a scrunched-up wad of paper," says Erasmus Twiddle. And he takes the soggy dumpling from Zug and hands it to Letty Faffenhuffal-Hefenfaffer.

"It's my soggy dumpling!" Letty yells in delight. "Oh, my precious soggy dumpling! Oh *mwa mwa mwa*." Which is the sound of Letty Faffenhuffal-Hefenfaffer kissing her soggy dumpling.

"You tricked me for a second, Zug," says Erasmus. "You made a fake soggy dumpling track that led out the cafeteria door to the playground. You wanted me to think the thief had escaped that way. Unfortunately for you, I found the soggy dumpling on the end of an elf's nose and three soggy dumpling tracks in a shady alley behind Snoots Waterford's grocery store—a spot you would have to pass on your way from the cafeteria to Snoots's."

"Must've been where I dropped the stupid dumpling," says Zug. "Nothing worse than stealing a soggy dumpling only to lose it ten minutes later. Not that I was ever going to eat the thing. I took it to teach Letty Faffenhuffal-Hefenfaffer a lesson. Every day I carry her stinking groceries. They're heavy and it's a long walk from the store to the school. I do something nice for her and she never gives me a quarter or anything for my troubles. Not even a fishsicle. I don't *have* to carry her groceries. I do it because I'm nice."

"You don't do something nice for a person because you want them to do something nice for you," says Letty Faffenhuffal-Hefenfaffer. "You do something nice for a person because it is nice to do something nice for a person."

"Yeah, whatever," says Zug and looks at his watch. "It's been lovely chatting, but I think I'll run away now." And away he runs to join the Navy. Several months later Erasmus receives a postcard from Zug. It says: *I stick my tongue out at you. Zug.*

"They say you can't have your soggy dumpling and eat it too," says Letty Faffenhuffal-Hefenfaffer. "But what good's a soggy dumpling if you're not going to eat it?" Letty cuts her soggy dumpling in two and holds one of the pieces out to our hero. "This is for you, Erasmus. I know it isn't a rainy day, but if anyone deserves to taste such a treat, you do."

Erasmus does not particularly want to taste such a treat, especially since it has been in Zug's sweaty hand, on the ground in an alley, in his—that is, Erasmus's—pocket, on an elf's nose, and Letty slobbered all over it with her kissing. He opens his mouth to say *No, thank you.* But Letty thinks he wants to be fed and places the soggy half dumpling on his tongue. It's not so bad. It tastes like chicken.

"I'd like to be alone with my soggy half dumpling, if you don't mind," says Letty Faffenhuffal-Hefenfaffer.

Erasmus does not mind. He walks out to the playground where he sees Lolly Gallagher, Mel Mel, and Frances Farkleberry. He marches right up to Lolly Gallagher.

"I'm not weird," says Erasmus Twiddle. "I'm just a not-detective trying to do my not-detective job, which isn't always easy."

Lolly's weather is mostly cloudy. But one of her clouds drifts to the left and reveals a tiny bit of her sun. "Oops," she says. "I seem to have dropped my notebook accidentally on purpose."

Erasmus picks up the notebook and hands it to Lolly.

"Thank you," Lolly says. The clouds over Lolly's head disappear and her sun shines so brightly that it hurts Erasmus's eyes.

"Run!" says Frances Farkleberry, and the girls run off, giggling.

"It's not fair," says Erasmus Twiddle. "I return the soggy dumpling to Letty Faffenhuffal-Hefenfaffer, I prove that the soggy dumpling thief is the soggy dumpling thief, and Zug escapes anyway. What kind of ending is that?"

Not a very fair ending, indeed. But the world is not always fair, not even for someone as famous and talented as Erasmus

Twiddle. It is possible, however, that Erasmus and Zug will meet again. Yes, perhaps this is not an ending at all, but the beginning of a long and not-very-friendly relationship between our famous and talented not-detective and the feared and loathsome soggy dumpling thief of Grmkville.

a Most Mysterious Mystery
proves not so Mysterious after all
or The Case of the Evil Weevil

It has been some time since we checked in with Erasmus Twiddle and the most mysterious mystery. Weevil Kneevil, you may remember, is being held at police headquarters in a jar-prison. Travis Plunkett, Frances Farkleberry, Dexter Dumfey, Nubs Carmichael, Georgiana Puckerbush, and Fred Zuplansky all think he stole their furgle, fleb, grumber, hojie, ploff, yonk, and oogoo. Our hero does not think Weevil Kneevil stole any such stuff, so he and Bagby Butterbottom are hiding outside Suzy Loopy's house, waiting for Suzy Loopy and her eebee to return from seeing the world's largest oven mitt.

"I will catch the thief as soon as Suzy Loopy returns and he tries to steal her eebee," says our famous and talented not-detective, Erasmus Twiddle. "That's why I'm hiding here."

Yes, well, Erasmus and Bagby have been hiding outside Suzy Loopy's house for quite a while now. Perhaps Suzy Loopy did not come straight home after seeing the world's largest oven mitt. Perhaps she decided to spend the night in the

146

oven mitt. Erasmus cannot save Weevil Kneevil if Suzy Loopy and her eebee do not return to Grmkville. Or can he?

"Bagby," says our hero, "you must pretend that you're Suzy Loopy returning from the world's largest oven mitt with your eebee. I need you to *act*."

"What is my motivation?" booms Bagby. "Am I an only childeth? Alas! What kind of relationship dideth I have with my dollies when I was younger?"

"Your motivation, Bagby, is to help me save Weevil Kneevil."

"Ah, yes!" booms Bagby. "Verily and forsooth! I will be a better Suzy Loopy than Suzy Loopy herself! Aaargh!" And with that, Bagby puts on his Suzy Loopy costumery, which he just happens to have with him.

It certainly must be admitted that Bagby does *not* look a whole lot like Suzy Loopy. Let's hope he acts better than he looks.

"Now, good Twiddle, I will fashion an eebee out of cardboard!" booms Bagby.

And it is a good thing that Bagby knows what an eebee is and can fashion one out of cardboard, because Erasmus certainly could not do it. Bagby finishes making his cardboard eebee. What is an eebee?

"Well, it's kinda hard to describe," says Erasmus Twiddle. "It's sort of . . ." He makes a bunch of strange hand gestures, "and then it's also . . ." He makes another bunch of strange hand gestures, ". . . and *that's* what an eebee is."

A buzzing noise. Why, it's Weevil Kneevil!

"Zounds! Do my eyes playeth tricks on meself? How is thou here, Kneevil?" booms Bagby Butterbottom in his Suzy Loopy costumery.

"I escaped," squeaks a breathless Weevil Kneevil. "I told Travis Plunkett and the others that I'd show them where to find the furgle and other stolen stuff. I don't know where the furgle and other stolen stuff is 'cause I didn't steal it, but I said I could take them to it if I wasn't stuck inside my jar-prison. They were going to tie a piece of string to me. They opened the lid of the jar and I employed a great many daring maneuvers and flew away. Erasmus, please help me. I'm not a thief."

"I know," says our famous and talented not-detective.

He gives the nod to Bagby Butterbottom, who struts out of hiding in his Suzy Loopy costumery and approaches Suzy Loopy's house. Bagby is doing an excellent job of acting like he's Suzy Loopy returning home from seeing the world's largest oven mitt.

Erasmus pulls a jar from his pocket, very much like the one in which Weevil Kneevil was held prisoner by Travis Plunkett and the others. It has air holes punched in the lid and everything.

"I thought you said you knew I wasn't the thief," whines Weevil Kneevil, who thinks the jar is for him.

But the jar is not for him. Bagby Butterbottom, at the front door to Suzy Loopy's house, sets the cardboard eebee on the ground and pretends to dig in his purse for keys. Erasmus takes off running, straight for him. Bagby Butterbottom smiles to himself and doesn't at all notice Erasmus rushing toward him. Nor does he notice that the cardboard eebee is inching away from him—or so it seems—all by itself.

"Oof begads!" utters a startled Bagby Butterbottom, as Erasmus at last closes in on the cardboard eebee and clamps shut his jar. He has caught something in the jar. It's a bug.

Weevil Kneevil takes one look at the bug trapped in Erasmus's jar and squeaks: "It's my long-lost cousin, Evil Weevil! Fly away!" Which is exactly what the courageous Weevil Kneevil does.

Neither Erasmus nor Bagby can fly, but I do not think that they would fly away from Evil Weevil even if they could. Especially since Erasmus has already captured Evil Weevil in a jar. Just in time, too, because here are Travis Plunkett, Frances Farkleberry, Dexter Dumfey, Nubs Carmichael, Georgiana Puckerbush, and Fred Zuplansky, and they are not very happy.

"Weevil Kneevil got away," complains Georgiana Puckerbush.

"You haven't been all that helpful in solving this mystery, Erasmus," says Travis Plunkett. "We've been doing all the work."

"I'm not helpful when it comes to capturing the wrong bug, no," says a proud Erasmus Twiddle. He holds up the jar with Evil Weevil in it. "Here is your thief. His name is Evil Weevil. I caught him trying to steal Suzy Loopy's eebee, which wasn't Suzy Loopy's eebee at all but only a fake eebee made of cardboard. And actually, Suzy Loopy isn't Suzy Loopy, but only Bagby Butterbottom dressed as Suzy Loopy."

"Fiends!" squeaks Evil Weevil from his jar-prison. "I'm still

149

cleverer than you, Erasmus. If I hadn't sent you that poem, you never would've caught me."

"Then I guess it wasn't too clever to send me the poem," says Erasmus Twiddle. "It will go easier for you, Evil Weevil, if you confess your crimes and show us where you've hid the stolen furgle, fleb, grumber, hojie, ploff, yonk, and oogoo. Remember: You've already admitted your crimes in the mysterious poem you left on my doorstep. I can match your weevil writing to the writing in the poem any time I want."

After much grumbling and buzzing back and forth in his jar-prison, Evil Weevil thinks perhaps it really will go easier for him if he tells Erasmus where he hid the stolen furgle, fleb, grumber, hojie, ploff, yonk, and oogoo. So that's exactly what he does.

"Here is your fleb," Erasmus says to Frances Farkleberry.

"That's my grumber," says Dexter Dumfey.

"Oh, yes, of course," says Erasmus, who really has no idea. "Here's your oogoo," he says to Fred Zuplansky.

"That's my furgle," says Travis Plunkett.

"Obviously," says Erasmus.

And so it goes until everyone receives just exactly what was stolen from them. But no doubt, after all that has happened, you are wondering what a furgle, fleb, grumber, hojie, ploff, yonk, and oogoo are. Well, they're sort of . . . but they're also kind of . . . and *that's* what a furgle, fleb, grumber, hojie, ploff, yonk, and oogoo are.

"Excellent Twiddle!" booms Bagby Butterbottom. "How couldeth thou and thee and then some be so sure that Weevil

Kneevil was not the villain and that Evil Weevil was? Besides the fact that Evil Weevil's nameth sounds a mite villainous! Begads and nonsense!"

"Well, Bagby," says our hero, "I kept thinking about the last line in the mysterious poem that Evil Weevil left on my doorstep. Evil wrote that the poem was my clue. But how could the poem be my clue? Then I saw it. Evil Weevil hid his name in the poem. If you look at the first letters of each line in the poem, you'll see that they spell out his name."

It is true. Here is the mysterious poem again, so you can see for yourself:

> Erasmus Twiddle thinks he's clever,
> Villains and thieves outsmart him never.
> Isn't he great, folks? I say, Pooh!
> Let evil reign, that's what I'll do.
>
> Wherever I go, trouble will follow.
> Every furgle and fleb and grumber and hojie,
> Every ploff and yonk and oogoo and eebee,
> Villainous villain that I am, I'll take them all—ho!
> I'll prove Twiddle's not cleverer than a shoe.
> Let's see if he can catch me. This poem's his clue!

"Peradventure!" booms Bagby. "That is one clever bug! Not a Grmkvillian, by any means, but a Grmkvillain if ever I saweth one! Forsooth!"

It is a good thing this most mysterious mystery has been brought to a happy close. It would not be all that swell for Erasmus Twiddle's reputation if he had been outsmarted by an Evil Weevil.

"No, it wouldn't," says our hero. "But luckily, Evil Weevil wasn't as clever as he thought and I was more clever than he thought. I'll keep Evil Weevil in his jar-prison in the center of town. Everyone will be able to see him there and he'll be a warning to any other weevils considering a life of crime who don't think I'm clever enough to catch them."

So, thanks to Erasmus Twiddle, this most mysterious mystery has proven not so mysterious after all. I do have one question, however. How could Evil Weevil write a poem since a pencil must be mighty heavy for such a little bug? Well, I suppppose that is another mystery altogether, and perhaps one day Erasmus will figure it out, but until then—

"Alas and wherefore!" booms Bagby Butterbottom, who wears a helmet over his Suzy Loopy costumery. "Weevil Kneevil's last stunteth was no big deal! I will make it through eleven apples *without* a weevilcycle or my name isn't Bagby Butterbottom!"

And with that, Bagby runs head first toward eleven apples lined up in a nice neat row. He is much too big to fit in an apple, of course. When he hits the apples with his head, well, all he does is squish them and make applesauce.

the case of the Puzzled Baboon

1

The wonderful thing about sitting is that you can do it almost anywhere: on a bench, a boat, a chair, a rock, a bed, a stair, a donkey, or a rabbit-hippo; in a tree, a house, a train, a plane, a car, a cave, a swing, or a sandbox. You can even sit on a shoe or in a giant anthill. You might not be very comfortable sitting on a shoe or in a giant anthill, but hey, if you would like to sit on a shoe or in a giant anthill, I am certainly not going to stop you.

The truth is, there are too many places to sit

and I cannot possibly name them all. But one place you should *not* sit is in the middle of a road. Any road. But especially a busy road. You could get hurt and you could also disrupt many important goings-on sitting in the middle of a busy road. Particularly if you are a baboon. The middle of a busy road is absolutely the worst place for a baboon to sit. Who expects to see a baboon sitting in the middle of a busy road?

So just think what trouble it is that a baboon has plopped down in the middle of not one, but *two* busy roads in Grmkville. The baboon has taken a seat in the middle of the busiest intersection in town, which is where he is now, scratching his head and looking puzzled.

Cars honk. Grmkvillians shout: "Get out of the two busy roads, you baboon!" But the baboon does not get out of the two busy roads. And it is not long before cars are lined up as far as the eye can see: traffic at a standstill in all directions, the important business of Grmkville brought to a halt.

"I thought I had a thought," puzzles the puzzled baboon. "But if I thought I had a thought, then . . . um, isn't *that* a thought even if it isn't the thought I thought I had?"

"Where did the puzzled baboon come from? Why is he puzzled? Why is he sitting in the middle of the busiest intersection in Grmkville?" asks our famous and talented not-detective, Erasmus Twiddle. Indeed, these are important questions—questions everyone in Grmkville is asking.

"Frankly," says No One in Particular. "I don't care where the baboon came from or why he's puzzled, as long as he sits somewhere else—in a park, say, where he wouldn't be a bother

154

to anyone except maybe a few pigeons."

"It's only a baboon," says Dexter Dumfey. "I can just pick him up and move him."

Which is exactly what Dexter Dumfey decides to do. All of Grmkville looks on as Dexter rolls up his shirtsleeves and approaches the baboon.

"Goodbye, I think?" the baboon says to Dexter Dumfey. The animal really means "Hello." You see how puzzled he is.

With a heave and a ho, Dexter tries to lift the baboon, but the animal is too heavy. Snoots Waterford and Woober Willoughby offer to help. Dexter, Snoots and Woober heave and ho but—

"Hee hee hee," laughs the puzzled baboon. "You're scratching me."

The creature really means they're tickling him. Which is *all* they are doing, because no matter how much Dexter, Snoots, and Woober heave and ho they cannot manage to lift the puzzled baboon.

"He must have weights under his fur," says Woober Willoughby. "We could get a crane to lift him if there wasn't all this traffic in the way."

"Shoo, baboon!" says Dexter Dumfey. "Shoo! Shoo!"

Why is Dexter Dumfey hissing the word *shoe* at the puzzled baboon? Everyone knows that puzzled baboons don't wear shoes. Does Dexter Dumfey think that puzzled baboons should wear shoes? Does Dexter Dumfey think that the puzzled baboon's feet smell and that he should put on a pair of shoes so they won't smell so bad? The puzzled baboon puzzles over this and smells his feet.

"A puzzled baboon with weights under his fur sitting in the middle of two busy roads and smelling his feet is a real problem," says Erasmus Twiddle. "If Grmkville is ever to be the same again, something must be done." And with that, our hero marches up to the puzzled animal. "I am Erasmus Twiddle," announces Erasmus Twiddle. "And you are a baboon."

"Do you think?" says the puzzled baboon. "Well, if you say so. Smell my feet."

Erasmus does not want to smell the puzzled baboon's feet.

"Smell 'em," insists the puzzled baboon.

If you ever happen across a puzzled baboon who insists that you smell his feet, you should probably do it.

"Yes," whispers Erasmus. "Puzzled baboons are strong and could hurt you if they become puzzled, *angry* baboons. So I will smell the baboon's feet, but I will hold my nose while I do it."

"Well?" asks the puzzled baboon, after Erasmus has smelled his feet.

"They smell like baboon feet," says Erasmus. Which gives the puzzled baboon something new to puzzle over. "I couldn't help noticing, baboon, that you look a little puzzled," says our hero.

"Do I?" asks the baboon. "What does a puzzled baboon look like? Like this?" And the baboon makes a very serious face that isn't at all puzzled-looking.

"No," says Erasmus Twiddle.

"Like this?" asks the baboon. And the baboon makes a face of surprise that isn't at all puzzled-looking.

"Uh-uh," says Erasmus Twiddle.

"Oh well," says the baboon. "I guess I'll never know what

a puzzled baboon looks like." And the baboon scratches his head, looking more puzzled than ever. "You know, Mr. Twiddle," says the puzzled baboon, "there *was* nothing that didn't puzzle me, but I think I've forgotten what it was, at least I can't remember what it was. It all goes back to me thinking I had a thought, you see . . . and, well, there you are. Or rather, here I am."

Erasmus is starting to get a little puzzled himself.

"I've forgotten why I'm puzzled," explains the puzzled baboon.

"Ah," says our hero, "so you're puzzled because you don't know what you're puzzled about. You must have lost a thought. Lucky for you, I'm a not-detective and good at finding lost things."

Perhaps you are surprised to learn that a puzzled baboon can lose a thought just as a person might lose a soggy dumpling. Well, if you are surprised, then you are surprised. There's nothing I can do about it. But a thought is a thing, just as a soggy dumpling is a thing, and things can get lost.

"I'll help you find your Lost Thought," Erasmus Twiddle tells the puzzled baboon. "Then maybe you won't be puzzled because you don't know what you're puzzled about and you'll get up from sitting in the middle of two busy roads."

The angry Grmkvillians stuck in traffic rev their engines.

"Out of the way, Twiddle!" shout the angry Grmkvillians. "We have important goings-on that need to get going and we aim to run over that baboon!"

It is mean to run over a baboon, puzzled or otherwise, and

Erasmus Twiddle will not get out of the way. Surely no one will run over our hero just to be mean and run over a puzzled baboon. Or will they?

2

The angry Grmkvillians glare and rev their engines louder than ever.

"My fellow Grmkvillians," calls brave Erasmus (who is perhaps not feeling as brave as he would like), "it isn't nice to run over a puzzled baboon, even if that puzzled baboon is sitting in the middle of two busy roads and causing all kinds of trouble. But it is even less nice to run over a famous and talented not-detective. Which is why I ask you to give me one day. If I can't get this puzzled baboon out of the two busy roads by tomorrow, I'll get out of the way and then you can run him over."

"Hey," says the puzzled baboon.

"Don't worry," whispers our hero. He makes a gesture which means *I won't let anyone run you over, baboon, not tomorrow or any day.*

"But we have important goings-on that need to get going," shout the angry Grmkvillians.

"Take a vacation," suggests Erasmus. "This will be Puzzled-Baboon-Sat-in-the-Middle-of-Two-Busy-Roads-and-Wouldn't-Get-Up Day, a new Grmkville holiday."

"Hmm. Okay," say the angry Grmkvillians, who, it must be admitted, are not so angry now that they are on vacation. They lock their cars and skip off to the beach.

"I'm not skipping off to any beach!" snorts Henrietta Humphreys, who is twice as large as she is rich. "The nerve of some baboons! As if there were anything for such a lowly creature to puzzle over! If I were a baboon and wanted a little attention, I wouldn't sit in the middle of any roads and pretend to be puzzled, I can tell you that! I wouldn't have to! I'd be a rich baboon, of course, and it isn't every day that people see a rich baboon, so I would always be the center of attention!"

"I feel bad for the puzzled fella," says Sam the Sidewalk Sweeper. "It's no picnic on a cleanly swept sidewalk to lose a thought. It happens to me sometimes and . . . and . . . what was I saying? Something about beans? Hello?"

"Losing a thought is weird!" cry Abel and Barry and Cindy and Darryl and Evelyn and Farrell and George and Harold and Izzy and Jared and Kevin and Larry and Mo and Nancy and Ollie and Perry and Quinn and Randy and Susan and Terry and Ursula and Valerie and William and Xavier and Yolanda and Zachary.

"The first thing we must do," Erasmus Twiddle tells the puzzled baboon, "is examine your ears. Everyone knows that a Lost Thought floats out the ear of the person or animal who lost it—although, according to the ancient wise man Barnabus Greazle, Lost Thoughts have been known to come out of a person's nose on occasion."

"Wrong-o, let's x m and m," says the puzzled baboon. By which I suppose the animal means something different than what he says, because he's very eager to examine his own ears. He pulls them toward his eyes but they are too short to reach.

He pushes his eyes closer to his ears, but all that does is give him a scrunched baboon face. It is a good thing our hero knows how to examine a puzzled baboon's ears.

"Hullo!" Erasmus calls into the baboon's left ear, and blows gently into it. "Hullo!" Erasmus calls into the baboon's right ear, and blows gently into it. And because the ancient wise man Barnabus Greazle did not get to be an ancient wise man without being wise (or ancient), and because a not-detective must be very thorough when searching for Lost Thoughts, Erasmus calls "Hullo!" into the baboon's nose and blows gently into each of his nostrils.

"Hmm. I don't see any sign of your Lost Thought," says Erasmus Twiddle. "No stray letters or anything like that. But your left ear, baboon, could use a good cleaning. I don't suppose we could go to the park and be puzzled?"

"Why would you want to be puzzled in a park?" asks the puzzled baboon. "Why would you want to be puzzled anywhere at all? It's no fun, if you ask me. Go afoot"—the poor baboon means *go ahead*, I believe—"ask me if it's any fun being puzzled. Ask me, ask me."

Erasmus does not want to ask the puzzled baboon any such thing. But what can he do? The puzzled baboon could beat him up. "Is it fun to be puzzled?"

"I refuse to answer such a silly question," says the puzzled baboon, and angrily scratches his head.

Things are worse than our hero thought. Clearly, the puzzled baboon will not budge until he is unpuzzled. Perhaps the animal wants to direct traffic and does not know it and that is why he is sitting in the middle of two busy roads. Erasmus gives the puzzled baboon a traffic cop's hat and a whistle. The puzzled baboon eats the whistle.

"Tasty," says the puzzled baboon. "I'll have you know, Mr. Twiddle, that I wasn't born to unloving baboon parents in a jungle too far from here or too close either. My mother's name is Mildred and my father's name is Ooh Ooh Aah Aah and—"

Uh oh. For some reason, the puzzled baboon is telling our hero his life story. A baboon's life isn't the most exciting thing in the world—a lot of swinging from trees and dragging his knuckles on the ground. And even as puzzled baboons go, this particular puzzled baboon has led quite a boring life until now. His life story doesn't have anything to do with *our* story, so we'll just sit here and ignore what he has to say. Who's listening to the puzzled baboon? Not us, no sirree. But boy can this puzzled baboon talk. Not that we're listening, because we're not, but . . . wait, I think the animal is finally getting to something important.

"—my auntie is having her yearly birthday bash," says the puzzled baboon, "and any baboon who's any baboon is going to be there. I remember loping along to my auntie baboon's house, minding my own baboon business and thinking how nice it would be if my knuckles didn't drag on the ground and I had a car even though everyone knows baboons can't drive cars because their feet don't reach the pedals, and . . . er, um . . ." The puzzled baboon shrugs and looks very sad and embarrassed because that is all he remembers.

"Hmm," says a thoughtful Erasmus Twiddle. "I wonder if your Lost Thought is floating around or if it's in someone else's

161

head. Just as a thought can float out your ears or nose, baboon, it can float *into* someone else's head through their ears or nose—which makes it harder to find."

This is too much for the puzzled baboon to think about. "It isn't very untiring being puzzled," says the animal. "I mean, it's not tiring being unpuzzled. I think I mean it's very tiring being puzzled all the time."

The puzzled baboon closes his eyes and starts to snore.

"Which gives me a chance to visit the Grmkville dump," says Erasmus Twiddle, "where all Lost Thoughts end up after floating around for a while—if they don't end up in anyone's head, I mean." And off our hero goes to discover what he can discover at the Grmkville dump.

3

At the Grmkville dump, Erasmus Twiddle knocks on a large Frangipani tree.

"Who is it?" call two voices from high up in the tree.

"It is I, Erasmus Twiddle, the famous and talented not-detective," says Erasmus Twiddle.

"We haven't been expecting you," say the two voices. "That makes you a surprise guest." And down the tree slide the Frangipani brothers—who, you may remember, always talk at the same time so it is lucky that each of them always happens to be saying just exactly what the other is saying.

"Don't tell us who you are," urge the Frangipani brothers. "Let us guess. You've come to sell us encyclopedias!"

"But I already told you who I am," says Erasmus Twiddle.

"Sssssh," say the Frangipani brothers. "We love surprise guests. Not many people want to visit a couple of brothers who live in a tree at a smelly dump and always say the same things at the same time. Would you like some tea? Someone threw out this mug and it has a little tea in it. How about a half-eaten hamburger? We have no idea who ate the other half."

Erasmus does not want any tea or a half-eaten hamburger, but the Frangipani brothers shove the tea and half-eaten hamburger into his hands anyway.

"You sell life insurance!" they cry. "You want us to sign a Save the Whales petition! You want us to make a donation to your charity!"

"I am here," says our famous and talented not-detective, "because a baboon has lost a thought and it is very important that I find it."

"Why didn't you say so?" cry the Frangipani brothers. "You'll find the Lost Thoughts in the Lost Thoughts section behind that large pile of tires over there."

They snatch the tea and the half-eaten hamburger out of Erasmus's hands, then plug up his ears with ear plugs and stop up his nose with a nose plug.

"You don't want anyone else's Lost Thought floating into your head by mistake," they explain. "Of course we'd be happy to purchase a set of encyclopedias, thank you." And with that the Frangipani brothers scuttle back up their tree.

Many Lost Thoughts float in the Lost Thoughts section of the Grmkville dump. They float above our hero's head but far enough beneath the clouds for him to read them. In fact, the Lost Thoughts float so far beneath the clouds that if Erasmus wanted to he could stand on a ladder and snatch any one of them he liked. PICK UP A QUART OF MILK. REMEMBER TO PAY GAS BILL. DO HOMEWORK. MY KEYS ARE ON THE KITCHEN TABLE. I WONDER IF I CAN LICK MY BIG TOE. There are quite a lot of Lost Thoughts here—yes, all sorts of boring thoughts that could belong to anybody.

"Bud nubbing thad seeb do belog do a baboob," says Erasmus, who talks in this funny manner because his nose is plugged up. But he is right. In all of these Lost Thoughts, there is not one that seems to belong to a baboob—I mean, baboon.

"I'b beginib do wunda ib I eber bind de—"

What? I'm sorry, but I have no idea what our hero is trying to say.

"I saib," says Erasmus Twiddle, taking the ear plugs out of his ears and the nose plug out of his nose, "I'm beginning to wonder if I'll ever find the baboon's Lost Thought. It's not at the dump, so it must be in somebody's head. But I'll have to talk to every single person in Grmkville to find out whose head it's in. I won't be able to do that by tomorrow when the angry Grmkvillians will be back from their vacation and ready to run over the baboon if he isn't out of the two busy roads."

This is not good, not good at all. Erasmus is starting to think that even a famous and talented not-detective might not be able to solve every mystery and not-mystery that comes his way. But what's this? Here's Professor Piffle with a whole bushel of bananas under his arm. He's eating the bananas one at a time, and very quickly, too, as if he has not eaten anything in a week.

"Hmm," says Erasmus Twiddle. "Professor Piffle is engaged in suspiciously baboon-like behavior. The baboon's Lost Thought must be in the professor's head."

Professor Piffle is indeed engaged in suspiciously baboon-like behavior. But so is Lolly Gallagher—who, you may remember, has her own weather (cloudy, partly sunny at the moment). If you look over there you will see Lolly sitting on a bench grooming Frances Farkleberry, which only means that she is picking little bits of something out of Frances's hair (*very* baboon). And there's Bagby Butterbottom hanging upside down from a tree in an eerily baboon-like manner.

"I have never seen so many people acting like baboons," says Erasmus Twiddle. "The puzzled baboon's Lost Thought cannot be in all of their heads at once. It has to be in one of their heads, but whose?"

Whose, indeed!

4

"**Out of the** three baboon-like suspects, I will talk with Bagby first," decides our hero. "Since I know Bagby best, I should easily be able to tell if he thinks he's a baboon."

"Ahoy, excellent Twiddle," booms Bagby Butterbottom. "It is good to see you. And may I say, sir, you taketh away the power of my nostrils!" Hanging upside down from the tree, Bagby tries his best to sniff. But his nostrils are stuffed up. "Woe be my nostrils!"

booms a sad, upside-down Bagby. "Oh nostrils, sniffing never-more!"

"You are aware, Bagby, that you're hanging upside down from a tree?" asks our hero.

Bagby looks around. "Why, it doth appear that I am! What do you know?"

"Baboons hang upside down from trees," says Erasmus.

"Verily they do!" booms Bagby. "Ahoy to hairy baboons everywhere!"

Erasmus looks very seriously at his upside-down friend. "Bagby, there is a baboon sitting in the middle of the two busiest roads in Grmkville. He is sitting there causing all kinds of trouble because he has lost a thought. I think maybe his thought is in your head."

"Oof," cries Bagby Butterbottom, falling from the tree. Standing right side up again, he booms: "Twiddle, dear fellow, I assure you that no baboon's thought is in my noggin! I am not feelingeth all that baboonish, as the saying goes! Aaargh and ver-ily, I was hanging upside down from the tree because I got tired of looking at things in the same way! Sometimes one needeth to turn the world on its head! Or should I say, turn one's selfeth on one's head so it *looks like* the world is turned on its head and . . . oh, peg leg! I willeth accompany you on your baboon adventure, if you don't mind!"

Erasmus does not mind, and off the two of them go to see Professor Piffle, who is still eating bananas and acting very much like a baboon.

"Just the not-detective I was looking for," says Professor

Piffle. "I can eat two bananas at once. Watch."

Professor Piffle takes two peeled bananas and shoves them into his mouth at once. It is very impressive to shove two bananas into your mouth at once, but you should not try it at home. You should not try it at school either. You should *never* try to shove two bananas into your mouth at once, because you could choke. You have to be a professor with fancy degrees from the best schools in the world to be able to shove two bananas into your mouth at once.

"Nonsense," exclaims Professor Piffle, when Erasmus suggests that the puzzled baboon's Lost Thought might be in his head.

"You *are* eating bananas in a most baboon-like fashion, sir!" booms Bagby Butterbottom.

"Bananas are brain food, a professor's best friend," explains Professor Piffle. "But if you want to understand this baboon business, you'll kindly take a look at these two charts I have with me." And Professor Piffle pulls two charts out from under his shirt, which look like this:

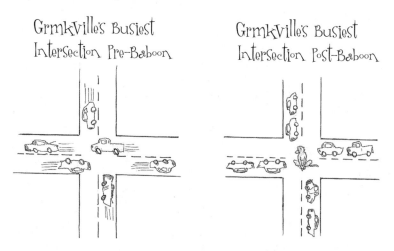

Grmkville's Busiest Intersection Pre-Baboon

Grmkville's Busiest Intersection Post-Baboon

"Now," says Professor Piffle, "you will note that before said baboon sat in the middle of two busy roads, there was no baboon sitting in the middle of two busy roads. You will further note that once this baboon sat in the middle of two busy roads—well, there he was. Now, baboons at rest tend to stay at rest. So if we multiply the weight of the baboon by the distance he doesn't travel and divide by the force of the cars that would otherwise be driving past if the baboon were not sitting in the middle of two busy roads . . ."

Professor Piffle writes a long and complex math formula on the baboon charts—a whole bunch of numbers and letters which, like the professor's banana-eating skills, should impress us quite a bit, even if we don't know what they mean. No matter, really. Since the Lost Thought does not seem to be in Professor Piffle's head, Erasmus and Bagby venture off to see Lolly Gallagher and Frances Farkleberry. The Lost Thought must certainly be in one of *their* heads since it is not in Bagby's or Professor Piffle's head.

"Are you calling me a baboon?" Lolly Gallagher asks Erasmus Twiddle. Her little sun disappears behind dark, rumbling clouds. When she saw Erasmus walking toward her, she thought he wanted to ask her out for ice cream and her sun had twinkled brightly behind hardly any clouds at all. "So I'm a baboon, am I?" storms Lolly Gallagher.

"No, I—" stammers Erasmus.

"Fair damsels!" booms Bagby. "Peradventure and woe! What my goodeth friend here is trying to sayeth is that there is a baboon where no baboon should be and—forsooth!—not acting like much of a baboon in the leasteth! And here thou art, gentle mistresses, acting more like baboons than yon baboon himself!"

"We aren't acting like baboons," says Frances Farkleberry. "I took a tumble in the grass and Lolly is just picking the blades of grass out of my hair, is all."

"Ah! Well, I think that explainseth everything!" booms Bagby. "What say you, Twiddle?" Bagby slaps our hero on the back and does not wait for an answer. "If either of you girls wouldeth ever care to ride in a land-pirate's bush-vessel, we are at your service."

Bagby bows. Lolly and Frances giggle. Lolly's sun reappears. She bites her bottom lip and glances at Erasmus, who is not very happy. He has talked with all three baboon-like suspects and is not any closer to finding the puzzled baboon's Lost Thought.

"Not any closer to finding the Lost Thought!" barks Henrietta Humphreys, the most well-to-do and well-fed person in all of Grmkville. "Disgraceful! It isn't safe on the streets anymore! One minute you're being carried down the avenue by your servants and the next minute you could think you're a baboon! Ugh! What is this town coming to? What are baboons doing with thoughts anyway? Next thing you know, they'll be demanding the right to vote or some such nonsense!"

". . . something about beans," says Sam the Sidewalk Sweeper. "I want beans? You want beans? Someone somewhere wants beans? Anywhich, I *am* glad the baboon hasn't started throwing his poop around. I'm sure some of it would end up on the sidewalks and I'd get stuck cleaning it up. If you've ever been to the zoo, then you probably know that baboons throw their poop when they're unhappy. It's kind of gross."

"Maybe the puzzled baboon wants beans?" offer Abel and Barry and Cindy and Darryl and Evelyn and Farrell and George and Harold and Izzy and Jared and Kevin and Larry and Mo and Nancy and Ollie and Perry and Quinn and Randy and Susan and Terry and Ursula and Valerie and William and Xavier and Yolanda and Zachary.

The sun sets over the horizon. Grmkvillians everywhere return to their houses and settle in for the night—Grmkvillians everywhere except for Erasmus Twiddle and Bagby Butterbottom, who pay a last visit to the puzzled baboon at Grmkville's busiest intersection.

"We'll see you first thing in the morning, baboon" says Erasmus Twiddle.

"'Til the morrow, hairy sir!" booms Bagby.

Someone has left a picnic basket of potato salad for the puzzled baboon, and all night long the animal sits in the middle of the two busy roads, scratching his head, looking puzzled and eating potato salad. And all night long, Erasmus lies awake in bed, thinking only that the puzzled baboon's Lost Thought is as lost as ever and wishing that tomorrow might never come.

5

Tomorrow does come, of course. Tomorrow is today. Yes, Puzzled-Baboon-Sat-in-the-Middle-of-Two-Busy-Roads-and-Wouldn't-Get-Up Day has passed, and here are Dexter Dumfey and the rest of the Grmkvillians climbing back into their cars, ready to get going on their important goings-on.

"What, still here?" shout the angry Grmkvillians who are angry all over again when they see the puzzled baboon sitting in the middle of the two busy roads, scratching his head and looking puzzled. "All right, you had your chance, baboon!" shout the angry Grmkvillians. "Now we'll squash you with our cars! Out of the way, Twiddle! You promised!"

Erasmus and Bagby stand with the puzzled baboon in the middle of the two busy roads.

"Ah, yes, I'm afraid I musteth be going!" booms Bagby, who looks at his wrist where a watch should be, except that he isn't wearing any watch. "Remember: Take this road for three miles, turn left, follow the wooded path over the hills and through the valley, and that's where the party is. You can't miss it."

The puzzled baboon stops scratching his head.

"What did you just say?" Erasmus Twiddle asks his friend.

"When, hark?"

"Just now. Something about a party. You gave out directions to a party." And turning quickly to the puzzled baboon, our hero asks: "Baboon, how do you get to your auntie baboon's house?"

The puzzled baboon thinks very hard, but no matter how hard he thinks, he cannot remember how to get to his auntie baboon's house.

"You have an auntie baboon too?" Bagby booms to the baboon. "Why, I have an auntie baboon!"

"Excuse me, Bagby," says Erasmus, "but you do not have an auntie baboon."

"I don't?"

171

"No. What you have is the baboon's Lost Thought, which are the directions to his auntie baboon's house." And with that, Erasmus takes his special not-detective Tweezer Thingie from his pocket. Then he pulls and yanks and yanks and pulls until the baboon's Lost Thought comes out of Bagby's left nostril.

"The power of my nostrils has returned!" booms Bagby, sniffing most heartily. "Ye baboon's thought had stuffed up my nose!"

The angry Grmkvillians are getting angrier and angrier. They rev their car engines. It is only a matter of seconds before—

"Ready, baboon?" Erasmus asks, and holds the Lost Thought close to the puzzled baboon's right ear. Whoosh! It is sucked into the baboon's head. The baboon blinks several times, stands, and suddenly does not seem like the same baboon at all. He is so sure of himself.

"Now I remember," says the no-longer-puzzled baboon.

"I'm supposed to turn left at this crossroads. I didn't know which way to go and I sat down here until I could remember. I'd better hurry or I'll be late for my auntie's party." He shakes Erasmus by the hand. "Thank you, Mr. Twiddle. I'll never forget *this*, I don't think. I hope not anyway. Who can tell? And as for you," says the animal, turning to Bagby and shaking *him* by the hand, "I know I can trust you with my thoughts anytime. Thank you."

"Tell your auntie baboon we say hello!" booms Bagby.

The no-longer-puzzled baboon promises that he will indeed tell his auntie baboon they say hello. Then he lopes off down the street, out of the middle of Grmkville's busiest intersection forever.

"Yippee!" shout the angry Grmkvillians who are not at all angry now they can at last get going on their important goings-on. They are already planning what they will do next year for Puzzled-Baboon-Sat-in-the-Middle-of-Two-Busy-Roads-and-Wouldn't-Get-Up Day.

"You know, Twiddle," booms Bagby Butterbottom, as he and our hero make their way to a bush-vessel where Lolly Gallagher and Frances Farkleberry wait for them, "I have been thinking, alas, and I do believeth it is when things go wrong and can be righted again, when baboons lose a thought and such stuff, that life becomes interesting!"

"Bagby," says Erasmus Twiddle, Grmkville's famous and talented not-detective, "I couldn't agree more."

if you Love your Donkey, set him Free (again)

Well, you have almost reached the end of the book, so you should be feeling pretty smart by this time. Plus, you can amaze your friends and their pets by telling them all about Erasmus Twiddle, Grmkville's famous and talented not-detective. But perhaps, after everything that has happened, you are wondering what sort of place Grmkville is to live in, what with their being so many mysteries and not-mysteries to solve.

"What sort of place is Grmkville to live in?" says Erasmus Twiddle. "Why, it just happens to be the best place in the world for a not-detective! Except maybe The Land of the Rabbit-Hippos. Sure, maybe Grmkville has more mysteries and not-mysteries than other towns—which means more crime and bad stuff—but there are also days—whole weeks even—when there are no mysteries or not-mysteries at all, and no work for a famous and talented not-detective like me."

It is true. Take this fine summer afternoon, for instance.

Mrs. Carbuncle putters in her garden while Paramus Plotz frolics in the yard in his donkey hat and hoof mittens. Mrs. Carbuncle has a lot on her mind, and after several minutes of puttering, she sets down her garden tools.

"Here, Paramus! Here, donkey donkey!" calls Mrs. Carbuncle.

Paramus Plotz trots up as fast as he can because he has become quite a well-behaved donkey. Mrs. Carbuncle pats him on the head.

"Paramus," she says softly, "I don't think you should be my pet donkey anymore."

"Hee haw!" cries Paramus, which is the sort of thing an upset donkey might say.

"No, I've made up my mind," says Mrs. Carbuncle. "You are much nicer than you used to be and you've been an excellent donkey, but let's be honest, you only have two legs and a two-legged donkey is . . . well, it's not the kind of donkey I had in mind for a pet. Besides, you should be out playing with other children."

"Hee haw," says Paramus, not quite as forcefully as before.

"I'm sorry," says Mrs. Carbuncle. "But I think it's for the best."

Paramus Plotz does not look as happy as you might expect him to look. The only reason he became a donkey in the first place is because he tried to explode Mrs. Carbuncle's first pet donkey, Reginald. He should be happy. Mrs. Carbuncle is telling him that he does not have to be a donkey anymore, which means that he is no longer punished. But Paramus likes being a two-legged donkey. He likes being a two-legged donkey even more than he likes being a boy.

"Can I keep my donkey hat and hoof mittens?" Paramus asks finally.

"Of course," says Mrs. Carbuncle. "And you can visit whenever you like. Now run along."

Paramus Plotz runs along and wears his donkey hat and hoof mittens everywhere he goes—school, home, yoga class. He visits Mrs. Carbuncle at least twice a week, where he hee haws as much as he likes and Mrs. Carbuncle pats him on the head and says, "Donkey want a treat?"

So life for Paramus Plotz is good. He gets to be a boy and a two-legged donkey. But life for Mrs. Carbuncle is another story. She lives alone, and on days when Paramus does not visit, she often sighs and stares at nothing for minutes at a time. What with Reginald the donkey off seeing the world and having his donkey adventures, and Paramus Plotz almost always doing boy things, Mrs. Carbuncle is a bit lonely. She has loved two donkeys and set them free. Certainly, setting them free was the right thing to do. But it is enough to make anyone lonely—especially Mrs. Carbuncle, since they were her donkeys.

Every single day, alone in her house, Mrs. Carbuncle makes Reginald's and Paramus's favorite dish—three cupfuls of grass with sugar sprinkled on top. And every single day, alone in her house, Mrs. Carbuncle sets a plate of this sugared grass in an open window and lets the breeze carry the aroma off to where Paramus plays and perhaps even halfway across the world to wherever Reginald happens to be.

If you look now, you will see the plate of sugared grass in the window. And here comes the rabbit-hippo, boogying past on his roller skates. The creature smells something delicious and sniffs and sniffs until his big rabbit-hippo nose leads him to the plate of sugared grass in the window.

"Hello," the rabbit-hippo says to the plate of sugared grass. He licks his lips and turns his big hippo head with its bunny ears left, right, up, down. "You are all alone," the creature says to the plate of sugared grass.

And because the rabbit-hippo does not like to see anyone or anything all alone, and because it is Sunday, he decides to eat just a little, tiny, eensy bit of the sugared grass.

"Mum mum mum," mums the rabbit-hippo, which is the sound the creature makes when he is eating something delicious. "Uh oh, ate it all," says the rabbit-hippo.

Yes, he certainly did. There is not a single blade of grass left on the plate. The rabbit-hippo is thinking that he's pretty thirsty after eating so much sugared grass when who should he see but Mrs. Carbuncle. He smiles and tries to look innocent, but it is no use. There are bits of sugar at the corners of his mouth and a blade of grass sticking out from between his rabbit-hippo teeth.

"Would you like some juice?" asks Mrs. Carbuncle.

The rabbit-hippo would like some juice very much. Juice is the very thing the rabbit-hippo was wishing for as he munched the delicious sugared grass.

"Oh, well, gee, I don't know," says the rabbit-hippo. "I've gotta get going and—"

"Come around to the sliding glass door in back," says Mrs. Carbuncle. "You should be able to fit through there."

The rabbit-hippo is suspicious. Perhaps it's a trap. But could one little old lady trap a great big roller disco-ing rabbit-hippo? I do not think so and neither does the rabbit-hippo. The great big roller disco-ing creature roller discos around to the sliding glass door in back and soon finds himself sitting in the living room with Mrs. Carbuncle, enjoying a glass of rabbit-hippo juice.

"I whipped up the rabbit-hippo juice especially for you," Mrs. Carbuncle tells the rabbit-hippo. "But don't worry. It's not made from rabbit-hippos the way orange juice is made from oranges."

The rabbit-hippo has never before heard of rabbit-hippo juice. He is flattered that Mrs. Carbuncle went to all the trouble of making it just for him. Unless there are other rabbit-hippos in the room and she made it for them too? He turns his big rabbit-hippo head with its bunny ears left, right, up, down. Nope. He is the only rabbit-hippo in the room.

"A toast," says the big creature, holding up his glass. But he cannot think of what to say, so he says "A toast to toast!" and downs the rabbit-hippo juice in one gulp. "You know, I'm not as lonely as I used to be," says the rabbit-hippo, who now has a rabbit-hippo juice mustache. "I've made many friends, although some Grmkvillians still move out of my way when they see me roller disco-ing toward them, and I wouldn't mind hopping once in a while. But really, I like Grmkville very much. I sleep behind Si Dobbler's pancake restaurant."

"Oh," says Mrs. Carbuncle, who can't imagine that sleeping behind Si Dobbler's pancake restaurant is very comfortable. Then she notices how late it is. "Why don't you sleep here tonight?" she suggests to the rabbit-hippo.

The rabbit-hippo looks at his comfy surroundings. He could fit quite snugly on the living room floor. "Okey-dokey," he says, and settles down to sleep.

The next morning, Mrs. Carbuncle awakens the rabbit-hippo with his favorite breakfast—three cupfuls of grass with sugar sprinkled on top and a glass of fresh rabbit-hippo juice. Mrs. Carbuncle and the rabbit-hippo talk and laugh and then Mrs. Carbuncle makes the rabbit-hippo his favorite lunch— three cupfuls of grass with sugar sprinkled on top and a glass of fresh rabbit-hippo juice. Mrs. Carbuncle and the rabbit-hippo watch game shows on TV, and before you know it, it's dinner time and Mrs. Carbuncle makes the rabbit-hippo his favorite dinner. I think you can guess what it is. That's right. It's steak au poivre. Then Mrs. Carbuncle entertains the rabbit-hippo with her collection of tree stump photos until she notices how late it is.

"Maybe you should sleep here again tonight?" she suggests to the rabbit-hippo.

"Okey-dokey," says the rabbit-hippo.

Night after night Mrs. Carbuncle asks the rabbit-hippo to sleep over, and night after night the rabbit-hippo says "Okey-dokey" until Mrs. Carbuncle does not have to ask anymore; the rabbit-hippo looks around the comfy living room and realizes that he is home.

The rabbit-hippo helps Mrs. Carbuncle wash the dishes. He helps her with her crochet. He can do everything that Reginald and Paramus used to do and even a few things that only a rabbit-hippo can do. And sometimes, when Mrs. Carbuncle goes to the store for milk and cheese, she tells the rabbit-hippo to take off his roller skates. She climbs onto his back and holds on to his bunny ears and they boom boom boom through town. This does not make everyone in Grmkville happy because the rabbit-hippo still cannot see very well when he hops and he crushes go-carts, wiffle balls, and lawnmowers with his hopping. Thanks to Erasmus Twiddle, the Grmkvillians are not as scared of the rabbit-hippo as they used to be, but that does not mean they are thrilled to have the big, strange creature around either. Not yet anyway. Still, while this loud hopping does not make everyone in Grmkville happy, there is no doubt that it pleases Mrs. Carbuncle and her pet rabbit-hippo—who, if they do not live happily ever after, will certainly live happily together for a long, long time to come.

cast
of
characters

Erasmus Twiddle

Date of Birth: That's classified not-detective stuff.

Favorite Foods: Peanut butter cookies, caramels, and cupcakes—not spinach-a-go-go or hamsicles dipped in chocolate, that's for sure.

Favorite Color: You will probably use this important information to pull off some devilicious crime. Silver, that's my favorite color. But maybe that's just what I want you to think. Just try and pull off your devilicious crime now. Ha!

Likes: Solving mysteries and not-mysteries, being a famous and talented not-detective, sea kayaking with whales in Patagonia.

Dislikes: Being asked if I'm a detective because anyone can be a detective. Being giggled over by Lolly Gallagher, Frances Farkleberry, or Mel Mel. Feeling grinchy, and talking in front of a lot of people.

If You Could Be Any Kind of Cheese, What Would You Be: That's classified not-detective stuff.

Bagby Butterbottom a.k.a. Andrew Michaels

Date of Birth: Hark ye! The date of my birth is my birthday! Aaargh, mateys!

Favorite Foods: Butterscotch pudding, FD&C Yellow #5!

Favorite Color: I'll tell ye, lassies, it is the brown of a land-pirate's bush-vesel, but it mighteth be different tomorrow!

Likes: Being me! I will now recite a few lines from the famous play *Macbeth Stubs His Toe:* "Ow! Ow! Darn toe! Is that a dagger I see before me? What do I care? I have stubbed my toe! Who put that step there?"

Dislikes: Not being me, you swabby woe-tellers! No doubteth you are familiar with these lines from the play *King Lear's Ear:* "What? What? I can't hear you! There's something in my ear! I don't know what it is but I don't like it! My three lovely daughters, show me how much you love me and I will give you whatever is in my ear!"

If You Could Be Any Kind of Cheese, What Would You Be: A most important question. If I couldeth be any kind of cheese, I would mosteth like to be a lump of toe cheese!

Mr. Jax

Date of Birth: I am five times older than my rubber chicken but only one-third as old as my collectible grandfather clock.

Favorite Food: Rubber chicken.

Favorite Color: The color of my rubber chicken, which is sort of . . . rubber chicken color.

Likes: When I am not sipping wine and flopping my rubber chicken in front of the fire, I like to take long walks in the woods and flop my rubber chicken. I also enjoy collecting collectibles: bronze thingamabobs, plastic whatsises, metal whodoyoucallits, wooden hootenannies, mugamug-whatchas, and hopping huh-huhmajigs.

Dislikes: Chickens that are supposed to be made of rubber but when you try to flop them you find that they are not made of rubber at all; they are made of some other stuff that is not half as good for flopping.

If You Could Be Any Kind of Cheese, What Would You Be: Floppy Rubber Chicken cheese, which is cheese that resembles a rubber chicken in its floppiness.

Rabbit-Hippo
(Rabbitpotamus)

Date of Birth: Hmm. I don't know. How about every Tuesday? Hippo hippo hooray!

Favorite Foods: Carrots and grass with sugar sprinkled on top. But I also like rabbit-hippo birthday cake every Tuesday.

Favorite Color: Blue.

Likes: Knowing that Erasmus Twiddle, Mrs. Carbuncle, Professor Piffle, and Dotty Polka are my friends. I also very much like candlelight dinners and bubblebaths.

Dislikes: Mean people, beets.

If You Could Be Any Kind of Cheese, What Would You Be: Rabbit-hippo cheese!

Professor Piffle

Date of Birth: I am like a fine wine that gets older with age.

Favorite Foods: I especially enjoy dining on carrots and bananas in my underpants.

Favorite Color: Purple.

Likes: To show everybody how smart I am. Ask me the hardest math question you can think of. That's it? That's easy. The answer is thirty-two. I also like to invent things, such as rubber chickens and roller skates for the Rabbitpotamus. I have been told that I have very kissable lips.

Dislikes: Silly questions about what I dislike.

If You Could Be Any Kind of Cheese, What Would You Be: In order to answer this question, I must ask a few questions myself. First: What do you mean by "if"? If, by "if," you mean "when" or "where" or "how" or "what," then you should rethink the question because it doesn't make any sense. Second: What do you mean by "you"? Is "you" the same as "me"? Is it the same as "I"? Am I supposed to be "me" or am I supposed to be "you"? If I am "you" then I cannot possibly say what kind of cheese I'd be, because I wouldn't be me; I'd be you! I know a lot of things, but I don't presume to speak for you, so maybe you should say what kind of cheese *you'd* be. And finally: If by "you" you mean "someone else altogether," well then, I'm afraid I you should not be speaking to me but to someone else altogether.

Mrs. Carbuncle

Date of Birth: My goodness, you'll think I'm terribly old. But I *am* terribly old! Dear, oh dear, I'm so terribly old that I've forgotten precisely how terribly old I am.

Favorite Foods: A wonderful prune–and–sour cream mash that is one of Letty Faffenhuffal-Hefenfaffer's specialties.

Favorite Color: Magenta.

Likes: Rabbit-hippos, pet donkeys (preferably four-legged), gardening, antiquing, and casually tight jeans.

Dislikes: Exploding animals.

If You Could Be Any Kind of Cheese, What Would You Be: I'd most like to be the kind of cheese that looks good in a pair of casually tight jeans.

Paramus Plotz

Date of Birth: Hee haw! (August 6th.)

Favorite Foods: Hee haw! (Cheeseburgers, grass with sugar sprinkled on top.)

Favorite Color: Hee haw! (Puce.)

Likes: Hee haw! (My donkey hat and hoof mittens.)

Dislikes: Hee haw! (Being without my donkey hat and hoof mittens.)

If You Could Be Any Kind of Cheese, What Would You Be: Hee haw! (Cheddar cheese. Duh.)

Reginald, the Donkey

Date of Birth: I am a donkey. Do you think donkeys know such things?

Favorite Foods: Grass with sugar sprinkled on top, ravioli, veal scallopine, grass with sugar sprinkled on top, filet de boeuf, grass with sugar sprinkled on top, chicken parmigiana, pommes frites, and grass with sugar sprinkled on top.

Favorite Color: The color of freedom.

Likes: All outdoor activities, including hiking, camping, and cross-country skiing. I also enjoy foreign films, taking strolls on the beach, and amusement parks.

Dislikes: Paramus Plotz, balloons.

If You Could Be Any Kind of Cheese, What Would You Be: That cheese with the little chunks of stuff in it. You know, it's kind of white or yellow and has those little chunks of stuff in it. That's the cheese I'd be.

The Furious Elf
(Ricky)

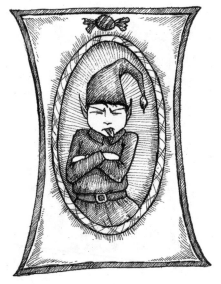

Date of Birth: It's not polite to ask a furious elf his age, you ninny!

Favorite Food: Humph! Who wants to know? Elf peppermints.

Favorite Color: Bah! What's it to you? Green.

Likes: Pfft! I know you are but what am I! Music, salsa dancing, rollerblading, tennis.

Dislikes: You! Come closer! I want to kick you in the shin! Also, leprechauns with mustaches who steal muddy boots full of elf peppermints.

If You Could Be Any Kind of Cheese, What Would You Be: Bah! What a dumb question! If I could be any kind of cheese, then that's what I'd be—any kind of cheese! Humph!

Letty Faffenhuffal-Hefenfaffer

Date of Birth: I was born on May 7th, exactly eleven days after my mother made her first truly soggy dumpling.

Favorite Food: My mother's soggy dumplings, fishsicles, liversicles and my numerous other frozen treats. Oh, and how could I forget about my tuna–and–pig feet casserole or my egg-and-lard burrito?

Favorite Color: A certain greenish-gray that forms on a slice of spinach-a-go-go when I leave it out for three weeks and it stinks something awful.

Likes: People who are funny with a great sense of humor, and people who have no sense of humor at all but are still funny. I'm not sure what I just said.

Dislikes: Zug, soggy dumplings that are too soggy or not soggy enough.

If You Could Be Any Kind of Cheese, What Would You Be: A cheese roll, which is a little bit of all the cheeses in the world rolled into one delicious ball. Mmm.

Lolly Gallagher

Date of Birth: Well, there's my official birthday, but that doesn't matter so much 'cause I didn't feel alive until the day I first saw Erasmus Twiddle. Erasmus and me, sitting in a tree. Oooooooh.

Favorite Food: Broccoli of love.

Favorite Color: Red, because it's mushy, mushy love color.

Likes: Erasmus Twiddle. ♥♥♥♥♥♥♥♥♥♥♥♥♥♥♥♥♥

Dislikes: Erasmus Twiddle when he's weird or mean. Sometimes I don't like having my own clouds and stuff. It's not easy being the only girl in school with her own weather.

If You Could Be Any Kind of Cheese, What Would You Be: Erasmus Twiddle's favorite cheese.

Zug

Date of Birth: Why should I tell you? Huh? What'd you ever do for me?

Favorite Food: It ain't soggy dumplings, I'll tell you that.

Favorite Color: Black.

Likes: Closed-minded, dishonest, uncaring, unfriendly, insincere people who don't want to have fun at all, ever.

Dislikes: Open-minded, honest, caring, friendly, sincere people who like to have fun.

If You Could Be Any Kind of Cheese, What Would You Be: Asiago cheese has a mild, tasty flavor that I enjoy.

The Puzzled Baboon

Date of Birth: What? Who? When?

Favorite Food: I don't dislike bananas, if that's what you mean. And potato salad. Potato salad isn't not good.

Favorite Color: Do I have a favorite color? I don't think baboons have favorite colors.

Likes: Auntie baboon's parties, sunsets, biking the Hamptons.

Dislikes: Being puzzled, seeing baboons, monkeys or gorillas in zoos, cows with attitude.

If You Could Be Any Kind of Cheese, What Would You Be: What kind of cheese do you want me to be?

The Frangipani Brothers

Date of Birth: St. Junkus Day, the Year of Our Garbage.

Favorite Foods: Anything that's been thrown out and ends up at the Grmkville dump: bread crusts, stale bagels, smelly fondue. If you've taken a bite of something and don't want it anymore, we'll be glad to eat it.

Favorite Color: We don't have a favorite color, but we have a favorite smell: us! We smell *bad*. Take a whiff. Go on. Do it.

Likes: Frangipani trees, junk, our Stupendous Sucker Machine, surprise guests, broken stuff, limbo dancing in the rain.

Dislikes: Taking baths or showers.

If You Could Be Any Kind of Cheese, What Would You Be: That's easy—rotten cheese. No one would want to eat us if we were rotten cheese and so we'd live a really long time. As cheese.

Weevil Kneevil

Date of Birth: Last Wednesday morning. I am a very mature weevil for my age.

Favorite Foods: Fruit, cotton, filet mignon.

Favorite Color: Orange.

Likes: To scare myself with too-dangerous weevil stunts. I hold the weevil world record for jumping over twenty buckets of angry goldfish on my weevilcycle. And I'll jump over twenty-one buckets of angry goldfish or my name isn't Weevil Kneevil!

Dislikes: Scaredy-cat weevils, whiners, my long-lost cousin Evil Weevil, cheese.

If You Could Be Any Kind of Cheese, What Would You Be: I said I don't like cheese.

Evil Weevil

Date of Birth: I *am* more clever than Erasmus Twiddle, you know.

Favorite Foods: Just because Erasmus Twiddle figured out my crimes and I'm stuck in a jar doesn't mean he's more clever than me.

Favorite Color: Maybe I *let* Erasmus Twiddle capture me. Did you ever think of that? It's true. I let him capture me. This is all part of my plan.

Likes: Making Erasmus Twiddle look foolish by outsmarting him, which I'll do soon enough. Sure, I'm stuck in a jar now, but I'll escape. Don't you worry.

Dislikes: Erasmus Twiddle.

If You Could Be Any Kind of Cheese, What Would You Be: Could you unscrew the lid of my jar a little? Loosen it a touch? Please? It's hard to breathe in here.

Henrietta Humphreys

Date of Birth: How dare you ask how old I am! I will never tell you. But I'll have you know that I'm older and wiser than you! Now I want to take a bath! Get me my loofah!

Favorite Food: All of it! But this is another rude question, to be sure! I only answered it to show you how nice I am!

Favorite Color: The color of money. Don't you have anything better to do than pester your betters?

Likes: Money, money, money! And telling my servants what to do!

Dislikes: Anything that isn't mine or can't be bought with *my* money, and anyone who isn't me! What a fabulous world this would be if it were filled with millions and millions of me! Can you imagine?

If You Could Be Any Kind of Cheese, What Would You Be: Expensive cheese!

Sam the Sidewalk Sweeper

Date of Birth: The third Thursday of July.

Favorite Foods: Prunesicles, soggy cereal, and soggy bread.

Favorite Color: The pristine gray of a cleanly swept sidewalk.

Likes: Good conversation, music, jazz, art, small villages in northern Italy. I am quietly intellectual.

Dislikes: Dirty, littered sidewalks. Especially sidewalks splattered with rabbit-hippo poop, donkey poop, elf poop, or any other kind of poop. If you are a pooper or a member of a pooper's party, please clean up after yourself.

If You Could Be Any Kind of Cheese, What Would You Be: Well, I *wouldn't* be filthy cheese abandoned on a sidewalk. People who buy cheese these days don't realize how leaving cheese on a sidewalk affects the cheese. It is very hard on a defenseless little piece of cheese. It's hard on me, too, since I'm the one who has to sweep it up.

Abel and Barry and Cindy and Darryl and Evelyn and Farrell and George and Harold and Izzy and Jared and Kevin and Larry and Mo and Nancy and Ollie and Perry and Quinn and Randy and Susan and Terry and Ursula and Valerie and William and Xavier and Yolanda and Zachary

Date of Birth: June 18th.

Favorite Foods: Apples and brownies and chocolate and doughnuts and eggs and fudge and grapes and hamburgers and icing and Jujubees and kale and licorice and Moon Pies and nectarines and oranges and pizza and quince and raspberries and snowcones and tacos and udon and vanilla and watermelon and xanthan and yogurt and ziti.

Favorite Colors: Aubergine and black and chartreuse and dun and ebony and fuschia and gray and hyacinth and indigo and jade and khaki and lemon and mauve and navy and orange and pink and quercetin and red and saffron and teal and umber and violet and white and xanthene and yellow and zaffer.

Likes: Foot massages and elephants.

Dislikes: Nitpicky people.

If You Could Be Any Kind of Cheese, What Would You Be: American and brie and cheddar and diet and emmenthaler and fontina and gouda and havarti and iberico and jarlsberg and kasseri and l'explorateur and mozzarella and new and old and parmesan and quark and roquefort and Swiss and taleggio and uniekaas and Velveeta and wensleydale and . . . and . . . hey, that's a lot of cheese. How about this weather we're having?

Woober Willoughby

"Rubber chickens—The Pets of the New Millennium! Rubber chickens—When You Care Enough to Flop the Very Best!"

Mrs. Mumuschnitzel

"We must see with our hearts and feel with our ears. I look equally beautiful in jeans or business attire."

Dotty Polka

"To roller disco well, you must feel the music. You must be the music. You are the music. I am not. You are the wind and I am a seagull. You—the ocean. Me—seaweed."

Snoots Waterford

"Would you like to see my snotty handkerchief?"

Mrs. Twiddle

"A potato sculpted into a pleasing figure is a more tasty potato."

Bill

"Je m'appelle Bill. Je ne suis pas français."

No One in Particular

No One in Particular could not be reached for comment. She thought I was a headless boober and ran away. Apparently, No One in Particular sees headless boobers everywhere. It's quite sad, really.

Mrs. Ploppityplop

"I'm a 'doer,' a people person. Everywhere I go, I hear people say, 'That Ploppityplop's a people person.' I hope those aren't my teeth I see in your mouth."

Fugsy B. Whicket

"Show me a picture of an ink stain and I'll tell you what I think I see. Ready. Go."

Noodles McDougal

"I am not a cowboy, but I am seeking cowgirls to ride the range of the infinite moment."

Hughley Hefenfaffer

"Yes, I understand perfectly, but only sort of. I mean, not at all. What? Sure, I hear what you're saying. Maybe. Who can tell?"

Suzy Loopy

"The world's largest oven mitt is about as exciting as a broken sprinkler. I'll take my eebee any day."

Travis Plunkett

"What day is it? What time is it? If you'll excuse me, I must put my furgle in my pants. And now I jiggle. Like so."

Frances Farkleberry

"Sometimes I like to close my eyes and imagine that I'm standing in front of a mirror taking a picture of myself standing in front of a mirror taking a picture of myself. I love my fledge."

Dexter Dumfey

"What is life without my grumber? It is a song waiting to be written, a poem yet unsung, a hamburger without a bun."

Nubs Carmichael

"Some call me Nubs. Others call me Stubs. Still others call me Frankfurter Phil. I don't really care what people call me as long as I've got my hojie."

Georgiana Puckerbush

". . . and the man said, 'Yoff and plonk? Goodness, my dear, what're those?' and I said, 'Not yoff and plonk. Ploff and yonk. And who doesn't know what a ploff and yonk are? Once you've seen a ploff and yonk, you'll know you've seen a ploff and yonk, believe you me.'"

Fred Zuplanksy

"I am humorous, huggable, and handsome. I'm your oogoo man. Who put the voodoo on my oogoo?"

Mel Mel

"My mom says that to know nothing well requires a lot of smarts. I don't know what she's talking about, but I got an A+ on my last homework assignment. It was called 'Gophers Need Good Dental Hygiene Too.'"

Mrs. Frumplebee

Unfortunately, Mrs. Frumplebee could not be reached for comment. She was so frightened by the lovely rabbit-hippo when he first hopped into town that she ran away. She's still running, farther and farther she goes, farther and farther and farther and farther . . .